THE MINX MINER

A Miners to Millionaires Story

JANELLE DANIELS

Dream Cache Publishing

Time travel and fairy godmothers?

When Gemma is offered the chance of a lifetime—to travel back in time and meet the love of her life—she jumps at the opportunity no matter how far-fetched it sounds. But when she's held at gunpoint after accidentally prospecting on one of Promise Creek's largest claims, she realizes her fairy tale might not end in a happily-ever-after.

Everyone wants Logan's wealth, but when he finds a woman—dressed as a boy—panning for gold in his river, he's intrigued. She claims she's a mail-order bride...but can't remember who her intended is. Gemma is unlike anyone he's ever met, and he wants her for himself—but as someone else's mail-order bride, she's off limits.

When the truth comes out, will he believe her? Or will she lose his trust forever?

To Dan.

CHAPTER 1

Excitement thrummed through Gemma Watts' veins as women filtered into the meeting room at the back of the bookstore. She was ready—more than ready—to change her life.

And tonight was the night.

She clutched her favorite book—the one set in a small mining town in Montana, where gold was plentiful and women were few. She'd always loved the miners in her stories, their excitement and thrill at striking it rich—and the mail-order brides they sent for and fell in love with.

Her heart warmed just thinking of them. She wanted the exact same for herself.

So when Dr. Lachele Simpson, a matchmaker turned fairy godmother, had explained what had happened to some of the women in book club and offered to send each of them to where they'd find the love of their lives, Gemma knew exactly where she wanted to go. 1880s Montana. The love of her life *had to* be there.

He wasn't in modern times. She knew that for sure.

She was twenty-six years old, lived by herself, had a small

1

catering business that wasn't doing so well, and had no social life except for this book club. She couldn't find a man who wanted the same things as her: to settle down, have a family, and enjoy the simple things in life.

The men she'd met just wanted to party or to experience the thrill of the chase over and over again in an endless cycle of short relationships.

It was so depressing! She wasn't sure what she'd done to get to this point in her life, but she was done with it.

Gemma wasn't one to languish over past mistakes, overanalyze her weaknesses, or regret her decisions. She was all about taking action, following her gut, and moving forward—and that's exactly what she was going to do.

Tonight, the moment book club ended, Dr. Lachele would send her to the past. It was already set up.

She had talked with her dad, and he knew she'd be traveling for a while and that he wouldn't hear from her. Sadness pricked her heart over leaving her father, but he would understand once he got the letter she'd asked her neighbor to mail in a few weeks. She'd explained it all in there.

More than anything, she knew he'd want her to be happy.

She pulled her bag in tighter under her legs so it wouldn't block the chair next to her. She had all the supplies she'd need to survive in the Wild West. Clothing, food, shelter, prospecting gear, a solar charger for her cell phone, antibiotics hidden in the hem of her dress, and enough gold—also hidden in the hem of her dress—to help her if an emergency arose.

This was going to work, she knew it.

She ran a hand over her denim shirt and jeans, second-guessing her choice in clothing, but then put it out of her mind. She had a dress in her bag, and, if needed, she could change clothes when she got there.

But her first order of business was to find more gold. She

knew where to look for large deposits, how to use her tools, and she had even traveled to Montana last summer to test it all out. It would be much easier to accomplish dressed like this. Skirts would only hamper her movement.

A chuckle pulled Gemma out of her thoughts, and she glanced up as her friend Rory sat in the chair next to her.

Gemma raised a brow. "What's funny?"

Rory reached over and tapped the worn historical western romance in Gemma's hands. "You. Are you sharing that book again? I think since you've shared it twice already, we should ban it. We've all heard how rugged and sexy miners are."

Gemma grinned. "Well, they *are* sexy."

Rory laughed. "I agree, but it's fun teasing you. They don't compare to dukes, though," she said pointedly.

"Always with the dukes." Gemma shook her head playfully. Her friend was obsessed with them. Rory read other kinds of Regency romance too, but she always circled back to dukes.

"They're the best. What more can I say?"

"Fine. They're pretty awesome." Gemma eyed Rory, taking in her fitted black pants and lace blouse. Her honey-blonde hair fell in loose curls over her shoulders, and her cornflower-blue eyes sparkled. She was almost the polar opposite of Gemma. They were both trim, but Gemma had thick, dark hair and hazel eyes. Rory looked polished and lux, whereas Gemma's appearance screamed salt of the earth—especially when clad in denim.

Although Rory appeared to have expensive tastes, Gemma knew she was poor. Gemma didn't know everything about her situation, but Rory worked hard—sometimes at two or three different jobs—trying to climb out of the mire her family had left her in.

Rory was one of the strongest people Gemma knew and one of the kindest. Which shocked Gemma even more, considering her background. If she'd had to deal with the same things Rory had, bitterness would have poisoned her heart.

Gemma cocked her head as she considered her friend. "What is it about dukes? I just realized I've never asked you." And this was her last chance to find out.

Rory tucked a curl behind her ear, looking away uncomfortably. "Because, even though other members of the aristocracy had money and land, dukes had the most power, the most influence. But more important, they fiercely protected what was theirs—including everyone under their care. They stepped up and did what was necessary, sheltered and protected those they loved, and provided opportunity for their tenants. If I could find a man like that, I'd never let him go."

Gemma leaned closer to her. "Will you take Dr. Lachele up on her offer, then?"

Rory bit her lip. "I don't know if I believe it. It seems almost too good to be true, doesn't it? I mean the others from book club are going *somewhere*. They haven't been back. But I just don't know."

Gemma understood completely. It was difficult to take things on faith, especially when life had been so hard. "I'm asking her to send me tonight."

Rory's eyes widened. "You are? After the meeting?"

Gemma nodded. "Yes. And if you want, you can be there. Watch me disappear, then you'll know it's true."

"But are you sure you want to go? I don't think the books we read are as accurate as we think. It might not be safe."

Gemma wasn't naïve. She knew things could go wrong. Horribly wrong. But to her, it was worth the risk. "I know. And I'm prepared." She patted the backpack under her seat. "I've thought of everything I could, prepared as much as possible." She shrugged. "But the bottom line is I want to do this. I want to see what it was like back then. I can't describe it, but I feel like I belong there. This is the right thing for me."

"You aren't worried at all? About anything?"

Gemma started shaking her head but then stopped. "My only worry is that I'll find someone who won't be faithful. That I'll fall completely in love and then he'll break my heart." She took a deep breath then smiled. "But with so few women, I hope that doesn't happen. I'm optimistic and prepared for everything else. It's worth the risk."

Although worry shone in her eyes, Rory smiled. "Then it'll be an adventure...*if* it works."

Gemma grinned. "It will. But I don't know how I'll make it through the rest of this meeting. I'm bursting out of my skin."

Another voice joined the conversation. "What? Do you have a hot date after?" Helen, one of her other friends from book club, crinkled her eyes in amusement as she took the seat to her right.

Gemma couldn't help but notice she was holding three books from different time periods. She looked at the books pointedly. "You couldn't decide which one to bring, so you brought all of them again?"

She arched a brow. "Why settle? If it's historical, it's worth sharing."

Gemma held up her hand. "No argument from me. Rory and I were just discussing which were better: miners or dukes."

"Dukes, obviously," Rory said, leaning forward and laughing.

"So she says." Gemma pointed her thumb in Rory's direction. "And no hot date. At least none that I'm planning on. It's possible though."

Helen looked at Rory, confused. "I don't understand."

Rory spoke softly. "She's taking Dr. Lachele up on her offer after the meeting."

"You *are*?" Helen's voice took on an excited edge, and she scooted closer. "I've been thinking about going somewhere too, but"—she tapped the three books in her lap—"how do I choose? Do I want a knight?" She held up each book in turn. "Or a prince? Or a suave millionaire from the 20s? How can you choose between such heroes?" She jokingly fanned her face. "If you ask me, you both have it easy. You already know what you want."

Gemma looked at her doubtfully. "I think you know what you want too."

Helen gave a small smile. "I know what I *don't* want, at least. I'm tired of men wanting me for my money or what I can give them. It seems all they see when they look at me is dollar signs. Whoever I end up with, in whatever time period, needs to have made his own fortune. Otherwise, how can I know he truly wants me?"

Rory frowned at Helen. "Do you really believe Dr. Lachele can do what she says?"

Helen nodded slowly. "I do. It's crazy, but I believe her. And if she can't"—she gestured around the half-empty room —"then where is everyone? Sure, sometimes people can't make it for a week or two, but not like this. It has to be true."

Rory huffed. "Or she's a serial killer," she muttered.

"She is *not!*" Gemma said with a laugh. "You'll see." She looked over at Helen. "And if you want to watch me disappear as well, you're welcome to." She raised her voice then and looked out at the room. "Everyone is welcome to come and see me go *poof* after the meeting."

At her announcement, Taylor swiveled toward her, leaning forward to see past Rory. "You're leaving tonight?" Excitement filled her eyes. "I'm thinking of leaving soon too. I'd love to see how it works."

Another voice joined the conversation. "I'd like to see it happen as well. Or rather, see if it happens at all," Penelope said. Gemma didn't know her as well as the others, but from everything she'd gathered, Penelope was a business shark. "It seems a little too fantastic if you ask me."

Rory nodded at Penelope, agreeing whole-heartedly.

Gemma grinned. "Join us then! It'll be my farewell party."

Rory and Penelope still seemed skeptical, but Helen and Taylor looked excited. At least, by disappearing in front of everyone, they would know it was true—then they could make their own decision about what to do.

❀

GEMMA THOUGHT SHE'D BE TOO EXCITED ABOUT LEAVING to be anxious, but as she watched Dr. Lachele say her good-byes to a few of the other girls after the meeting, she wrung her hands in front of her. It didn't matter that this was the right choice or that she was prepared.

She was about to change *everything*.

Permanently.

Perhaps it was all right to be a little anxious. She was ready to move forward. Her happily-ever-after was waiting.

Dr. Lachele walked over to her, her curled, shiny, purple hair bouncing with each step. Kindness shone in her eyes, and it immediately put Gemma at ease.

"Looks like you're ready to leave." Dr. Lachele smiled as she glanced to the bag slung over Gemma's shoulder. "You have a period-appropriate dress in there?"

"I do. I'm all prepared."

Her smile deepened. "I can see that." Her attention then turned to the other four women. "Hello, ladies! I didn't get a chance to talk to you before the meeting. I hope you're all doing well."

JANELLE DANIELS

Each of the girls assured Dr. Lachele they were fine before Gemma caught her attention again. "They wanted to be here when it happened."

"Ah, I see." Understanding lit the matchmaker's eyes. "I haven't sent anyone through time with others around, but I don't see why it would make a difference. The more the merrier!"

"That's exactly what I thought. Might as well make it a party." Gemma laughed.

"I love that." Dr. Lachele rubbed her hands together, and Gemma could feel the woman's excitement. "Let's get down to business. You want me to send you to find the perfect man for you." She glanced down at the book still clutched in Gemma's hands. "One in the Wild West?"

"Preferably in 1880s Montana. But if he's not there," she added quickly, "I will go wherever he is."

Dr. Lachele tapped her lip. "I have a feeling you're right. 1880s Montana is the right place. I can feel it."

Gemma didn't know if that's how it worked for the others, but she didn't care. Her excitement built until she thought she would burst.

"Are you ready?" Dr. Lachele asked.

"I am."

"Good. Hurry and say your goodbyes. This happens fast." She stepped back to allow the other book club members to wish her well.

She quickly exchanged a few words with Taylor, Penelope, and Helen. But when Rory hugged her, her chest tightened.

"Be careful," Rory said one last time. "I'm rooting for you."

Gemma pulled back, swallowing a lump in her throat. "I'm rooting for you too. You deserve love, Rory. Go after it. I bet there's a duke waiting for you." She gave her friend a wink to lighten the mood.

Rory chuckled before stepping back. "If I knew that for sure, I'd leave in a heartbeat."

Gemma hoped her friend took the leap.

Taking a deep breath, she turned back to Dr. Lachele. "I'm ready. Let's do this."

The others moved back to let Dr. Lachele get closer. "Things are going to turn out so well for you, Gemma. I can feel it. Now, to make it official, I need you to say the words. I wish..." She lifted her eyebrows encouragingly.

Gemma's heart thundered. This was it. No turning back. No second-guessing. "I wish to go back in time and meet the love of my life."

Dr. Lachele's smile widened. "Have a wonderful time, dear." She twitched her nose, the lights flared, and a moment later—

Gemma landed in the middle of a river.

CHAPTER 2

G emma gasped as icy cold water saturated her clothes. The current sucked her down, tugging at her bag until she worried it would break free. *Oh no you don't!* She would *not* lose her bag.

She kicked hard, using the adrenaline coursing through her to fight through the cold. Years of swim training helped her move before her brain could fully function, and she freestyled her way to the edge. The current was calmer here, and she pulled herself out, falling to her back on the bank.

Her chest heaved, not from the exertion, but from the shock of what had happened. She'd been dumped in the river! So much for her plans about what to do upon arrival.

My phone!

Whipping her bag to her lap, she opened it, grateful to see the plastic bags she'd used to pack the sensitive items had remained sealed tight. They'd even worked traveling through time.

Maybe the company could use it as a selling point.

She snorted and lay back down now that she knew her belongings were safe.

She was chilled from the freezing river, and, after a few minutes, she realized she'd have to do something about it. Inside the bag, her dress was also wet, but she hoped the antibiotics were still wrapped tight. She'd either have to strip down and hang her clothes by a fire or risk the cold and let them dry on her.

She was tempted to go sans clothes but didn't dare.

She scanned the thick foliage shielding her on the bank and stilled. The incessant honking that plagued her ears in New York City had vanished. Only the sound of bees in the wildflowers behind her and the occasional call of a bird in its nest could be heard.

The air was clean—unlike anything she'd ever breathed. Even when she'd traveled to Montana in her time, it hadn't been like this. It was so pure it was almost sweet!

She closed her eyes and ran her hands along the grass that enveloped her. Silky and strong, it rustled as wind moved through it.

She was alone. Utterly and completely.

Tears filled her eyes, but she pushed them away. She'd miss everyone she left, but she'd come to find someone even more important. And finding him would make the sacrifice more than worth it.

Taking a deep breath, she pushed herself up from the bank, grabbed her backpack, and moved toward a clearing that wasn't far off. Hopefully, she'd find dry kindling and could make a fire.

That was her first priority right now. After that, she'd scout out the area, make sure no one was around, and then start testing the water.

With any luck, she'd find a rich deposit soon and then head to the nearest town to claim it.

As long as she focused on her list of tasks, everything would be all right. She was going to make this work.

There was no going back now.

Logan Walburn rode across his land without seeing any of it. His mind swirled, overwhelmed by the news that the claim his father and mother had founded, one of the oldest and richest in Promise Creek, Montana, had a second mother lode.

It was astounding, mind blowing, and he didn't know how to process it.

His mother and father had brought him here when he was just a child, hoping to strike their own fortune.

And they had.

Neither of them could have known how much gold was concentrated on their land, how rich they'd become. Unfortunately, his father had never realized it, dying when Logan was eight years old.

But his mother, the strongest person he knew, had somehow held the land and fought off every prospector who'd tried to take it from her. She was a woman with grit, and he'd never met her equal.

No matter what problems she'd faced, no matter the difficulties, she'd held strong. And once he was old enough, he'd stood right beside her, protecting their legacy.

His mother didn't manage the mine anymore. He'd taken on all the responsibility of running it, allowing his mother to live the life of peace and luxury she deserved.

He just wished she would lavish herself with a few more luxuries. Most of the time she acted as though she still had to watch every penny she spent. But those days were long past.

He couldn't wait to tell her about this new finding. But with the exciting news came hard decisions. Everyone would know soon, and this type of find would bring people wanting to take it.

They'd need to add extra precautions and be watchful, wary. He just hoped they had enough time to put things in place before the scavengers came.

He looked up at that thought, his eyes narrowing at a small trail of smoke next to the river. He stopped his horse, contemplating it, and finally decided it had to be a trespasser.

Grimly, he took the rifle out of his saddle holster, grateful he'd taken it on the impromptu ride. Whoever it was would regret crossing onto his land.

As he approached the tree line, he slowed his mount, quietly making his way through the brush to the trespasser's campsite. He stopped for a moment, watching for movement, but when there was nothing, he moved forward into the clearing, dismounting quietly while still holding his weapon at the ready.

The fire was dying, but there was a brown, new-looking pack next to it. He was tempted to go through the items inside, but he didn't want the owner to spot him.

He scanned the area, still seeing no sign of the trespasser, so he walked toward the water, finding a young man, possibly a boy, panning for gold.

Anger wove through him. This was *his* land.

He cocked the hammer back, and the sound pierced the air.

The boy froze, but before he could turn around, Logan stopped him. "Don't make any fast moves."

The boy raised his hands in the air.

"Good. Now, stand up and turn around slowly. Keep your hands in the air." Logan hadn't anticipated capturing a poacher on his land and the subsequent ride to the sheriff, but it looked as though he'd need to detour into town.

As the trespasser stood up, Logan noticed the denim

pants and shirt covered a slim figure. Definitely a boy. "Turn around."

The boy hesitated, and Logan took a step forward. "I said, turn around."

As if realizing he had no choice, he turned but kept his face lowered so Logan could only see the cap on his head. "You're trespassing."

The boy's hand clenched into a fist. "I'm sorry. I didn't know this land was taken."

His voice was higher than Logan expected, but he didn't believe a single word. "How could you not know? This claim is well known to everyone in the territory."

He shrugged. "I'm not from this area."

That hardly mattered. "It's a crime to prospect on other people's land. I'll be turning you over to the sheriff."

"Please don't! I'm sorry. I'll just go. Please."

His stomach dropped, realizing that even a young boy wouldn't speak that way. Lowering his gun, he marched over and ripped the trespasser's hat off.

Thick, dark curls cascaded down her shoulders, settling at her waist. He gasped. "You're a woman!"

Hazel eyes connected with his, sparking with intelligence and fire. "I am."

He gazed at her form, wondering how he'd missed the curves of her hips and chest or where her shirt nipped at her waist. In no way was this a masculine form, and he swallowed hard, forcing his eyes away.

When he looked at her eyes again, she arched a brow, completely calm after his perusal. If he'd done that to any of the women in town who'd chased after him, they would've gone into hysterics.

"What are you doing here?" he asked, trying to revert to neutral ground.

"As I said, I didn't realize this was your land. If I'd known it was already claimed, I wouldn't have dared." She gestured to the area around them. "There was no one around, and I assumed it was free."

He frowned. "The territory is vast, but all the land around town is claimed. You'd have to know that."

She bit her lip and shook her head. "I didn't realize I was even near a town."

"Then where did you come from? You couldn't have just dropped out of thin air."

Her lips trembled as if she were trying to hold back a smile, but he couldn't imagine why a person would laugh in such circumstances—unless she was daft.

But she didn't *look* crazy.

She smoothed her features and stood a little taller. "I didn't realize I was so near town because the stagecoach I was on was attacked. I jumped to escape, unaware of where I was."

His jaw dropped, and he quickly looked over her again. "And you're well? You suffered no injuries?"

She shifted. "I rolled as I hit the ground. And I made sure to jump on soft-looking grass."

He didn't think such a thing would make much of a difference. But if what she said was true, it was a miracle she'd survived. "What happened to the other passengers? The driver?"

She winced. "I don't know."

"Did no one else jump?"

"Not with me."

Realizing she wasn't a threat, he hooked the rifle strap over his shoulder so it rested behind him. Her eyes widened at the move, and she did a little perusing of her own, her gaze lingering on his shoulders and chest before moving all the way down and back. Her eyes were warmer as they met his, and then she blushed. "Sorry. I couldn't help it."

"Couldn't help what?" His mouth was dry. Why had such a thing affected him so much?

"Uh..." She gestured at him. "I mean, never mind." He thought he heard her mumble, "Not appropriate, Gemma."

He cleared his throat, trying to focus on the situation again. "Where were you heading? On the stagecoach?"

"Which town is nearby?"

"Promise Creek."

She held up her index finger. "That's right where I was going. How fortunate!"

He frowned. "What business do you have there? Were you traveling alone?"

"Oh, um." She took a moment before answering. "Yes. I was alone. I'm here as a mail-order bride."

A lead ball settled in his gut. She'd already agreed to marry another? He didn't know why the news should affect him so, but it did. For the first time, a woman had intrigued him enough to want to know more about her. He'd courted a few of the women in town—mainly to appease his mother—but none had interested him.

The woman before him was gorgeous, confident, and, from the looks of things, knowledgeable. That wasn't her first time panning, and the fact she was out here, doing it alone, spoke volumes about her character.

He cleared his throat. "Who is your fiancé?"

"My fiancé..." She spoke slowly. "My fiancé is..." She turned away and rubbed her head.

He frowned. "Is something the matter?"

"No. I feel fine. Maybe a little headache." She looked at him. "The thing is...I don't remember who he is."

"You don't remember who you're supposed to marry?" He couldn't imagine such a thing.

She pressed her lips together. "Yes. We didn't write very

many letters before I set out this way. And you see, with the stagecoach robbery, my trunk was taken as well. My letters with his name were in them." She looked away as if embarrassed.

"I see." Had she hit her head, lost her memory, and just didn't recall the injury? "You can't remember anything? His profession? The location of his home?"

"No. All I remember is Promise Creek. That's where I'm supposed to be. I know it."

A terrible part of him, one he pushed away the moment he realized what was happening, was glad she couldn't remember. If she couldn't remember, she didn't truly care for her intended.

But people married for reasons other than affection all the time. This woman was off-limits to him no matter how attracted he was.

She might not remember who she was supposed to marry, but Logan bet the man waiting for her did. The minute she stepped into town, her fiancé would claim her. "If you'd like, I can take you to town," he offered. It was the right thing to do.

Her head jerked up. "No! I mean. No, thank you. I'm not ready to meet him yet."

"I don't understand." He looked at her clothing again and made assumptions. "If you need proper attire, I'm sure we can find something for you."

She looked down at her denim clothes. "You mean a dress, don't you?"

"Yes." How hard had she hit her head?

"I have one in my pack. It's probably a wrinkled mess." He must have looked confused, because she added, "I fell in the river. Everything got wet."

His heart skipped a beat. "You fell into the river, and you made it out?" He looked at the calm water in this area, but he knew that just a bit farther from here, the rapids were strong and would drown even the strongest swimmer.

"Fortunately, I was wearing this. I don't think I would have made it out in a dress," she said softly.

He didn't either. It was a miracle.

She let out a long breath. "Look, I'm exhausted. I don't know the man I'm meeting. I don't know anyone."

The need to protect her rose within him. "I can take you to stay with my mother." He winced. Maybe not the most accurate way of putting it, but he didn't want her to get the wrong impression. Staying with his mother technically meant she would also be staying with him. "I bet she would enjoy the company for a day or so while you recover from your experience."

She looked around the clearing as if weighing her options and laced her fingers in front of her. "What did you say your name was?"

Right. He'd seen her, held a gun on her, and hadn't properly introduced himself. "Forgive me. I'm Logan Walburn."

She smiled. "I'm Gemma Watts."

He wanted to take her hand and place a kiss on the back of it in a courtly gesture, but he didn't give in to the impulse. "It's a pleasure to meet you, Miss Watts."

Her smile widened slowly until she was grinning at him.

"What is it?" he asked.

"Nothing. I've never met anyone quite like you before, I think."

He didn't know what to say to that, so he just nodded. "I'll take that as a compliment."

"Oh, it is. Most definitely."

That was encouraging. "Good. Then what would you like to do, Miss Watts? Would you like a ride to town, or would you prefer to be a guest of my mother for a day or two?"

"A guest of your mother if you're sure she won't mind."

"Not at all." Their house was gigantic. If his mother wanted, she would never even have to see Gemma. But he had a feeling Gemma and his mother would get along just fine.

He bent down to take her bag, and she stepped forward. "Oh no. That's okay. I can carry that."

When she held her hand out for the bag, he handed it to her. "It's really no trouble."

She slung it over her shoulder. "I appreciate the offer. It's just...this is all I have left."

She'd lost everything else when the stagecoach was robbed. Of course. It made complete sense. Before Logan turned her over to her fiancé, he would purchase whatever she needed. He didn't care if she demanded ten dresses, he'd get them for her without blinking. "I understand. Why don't we head out before it gets late?"

He headed toward his horse, and he heard her follow until they cleared the brush and his mount came into view. At her soft squeak, he turned toward her. "What is it?"

She pointed at his horse. "Are we riding on that?"

The question was so outrageous he couldn't help but smile. "Yes. I don't generally take a wagon unless I'm going to town for supplies. We can ride double if you don't mind."

She shifted from foot to foot but didn't move any closer to the horse.

Realizing something was truly wrong, he retraced his steps until he was only a few feet from her. "What's the matter? You aren't afraid of horses, are you?"

"Not afraid, exactly." She looked into his eyes then, and the sun brought out a bright yellow ring around her pupil he couldn't look away from. "I've just never ridden on one before."

Her words finally cleared the haze from his mind. "You've

never ridden a horse?" He couldn't hide the astonishment from his voice.

"No. It's terrible, right?"

"Not terrible. Just astonishing." Then again, she was probably from a larger city. She probably had walked everywhere or ridden in a carriage. "I can teach you, if you'd like."

She brightened. "I'd like that. Seems like I'll need to learn now that I'm here."

Reality returned. She belonged to someone else. He had no right to offer to teach her anything. "Or, um, your fiancé could, I'm sure."

She dimmed. "Oh. Yes. I'm sure he could." She straightened and smiled. "Thank you for the suggestion.

She marched over to the horse as if determined not to be afraid. But she didn't touch the animal as she looked him over. "What's the best way to get on?"

He could give her instructions on how to put her foot in the stirrup and pull herself up. But he couldn't stop himself from touching her.

"Like this."

He stepped into her space and placed his hands on her waist. Her eyes widened and her gaze went from his chest up to his eyes. "Oh," she breathed out softly, shivering.

His heart thumped harder at her reaction, and his body itched to pull her close instead of putting her up on the horse.

But before he could make the choice, he was already lifting her into the saddle.

No matter what he wanted, she didn't belong to him.

He needed to remember that.

CHAPTER 3

Gemma couldn't decide which was more shocking—that she was riding on a horse across vast, open land or that her back was pressed up against the handsomest man she'd ever seen.

Seriously. Thor has been demoted to second-hottest man in the world.

Logan was the type of man she always envisioned in the novels she'd read, but even then she'd known that such a person couldn't possibly exist.

No real person was truly like the men in romance novels. But if anyone could come close, it was the hunky, muscled guy behind her.

It'd taken every ounce of willpower not to drool once he'd spoken with her and lowered his weapon. The way he sounded and looked, his manners and masculinity, everything about him attracted her.

His clothes weren't overly fine, but his horse looked—horsey. She snorted. She had no idea what made a horse quality or not. But she was impressed that it was able to move at all with both of their weight on top. Could all horses do that?

She wished she could tell him the truth—that she was from the future—but who would believe such a thing? *She* hardly believed it.

The horse moved faster beneath them, and she weaved precariously atop the saddle, unable to find her balance quickly enough.

His arm snaked around her waist, pulling her firm against him, and her heart knocked against her chest.

"Lean against me. It will make things easier," he said directly into her ear.

She shivered as his breath caressed her neck.

His scent of sandalwood and healthy male wafted to her, and she thought she'd die of bliss. She'd never been this aware of another man, and she wanted even more.

She did as he asked, leaning completely against him. But instead of feeling awkward, it felt comfortable. Right, even.

She thought he'd remove his arm from around her waist, but he didn't. He kept it there, curled around her, to keep her steady.

She knew he was just being practical—he probably thought she would fall off and break her neck if he let go—but she relished the feeling.

This was why she'd come here, why she chosen this era. She wanted a simple, easy-going, protective, and rugged man.

Logan was all of those things.

And maybe this was how it worked. Maybe Dr. Lachele dumped her here because she knew Logan would find her. Gemma wanted someone she could have a life with, stake a claim with, and build a future with.

She could envision it all with him. He might be working someone else's claim or maybe just protecting it, but she knew how to find gold. And if she could just orient herself, she knew *exactly* where the richest deposits were.

Everything she'd dreamed of, everything she'd wanted, was right here.

He cleared his throat, and when he spoke, she could feel the rumble from his chest against her back.

"I know you said you had a dress already, but if you'll allow me, I can supply you with the other necessities you'll need before meeting your groom."

"That's very kind of you." She wasn't quite sure what to say. Should she admit she'd lied about being a mail-order bride? He'd need to know if they would ever have a future together, but how would she explain things? She didn't know him well enough to know how he would react. "I don't need much." She didn't want him thinking she was a high maintenance kind of woman. "I have most of what I need in my bag."

Truly, she didn't need much, and from his clothes, she guessed he didn't have much to share. The finer things in life could come later.

"That was smart to pack the necessities in something you kept with you."

She chuckled. "I learned that the hard way. Last time I went on a trip, my suitcase—I mean my trunk—got lost."

"You've lost all your belongings before?" He sounded shocked at such a thing.

"Not all of my things. Just some clothes and stuff." It really hadn't been that big of a deal, but to him clothes were expensive. The loss of so many things would be a hardship in this time. She needed to remember that. "It was a long time ago."

She felt him nod, but he didn't say more.

"Does your mother live far?" she asked, wanting him to

speak more. She wasn't embarrassed to admit she was a little in love with his rich baritone already.

"Not too far. We should be there shortly."

"How close to town is she?"

"Approximately thirty minutes on horseback. The wagon takes a little longer."

Not bad at all. It could take an hour to travel a couple blocks in New York if the traffic was bad enough. Riding a wagon through gorgeous countryside? Yes, please! "How long have you lived here?"

"My parents came to make their fortune when I was very young."

"So you grew up here?" She couldn't imagine such a childhood. Mining wasn't easy in modern times, but it was much worse now. "What was it like?"

She felt his shoulders move slightly. "There were some hard times, but it wasn't too bad. Much different than back East, I'm sure."

That probably went without saying. Although, she didn't know what life was like growing up in the East during this time period either. It didn't seem like anyone had an easy life. Children worked in factories, there was little education, and hardly any medical care.

Her father owned a dental office, and just the thought of what dentistry was like during this time made her shiver. She was determined to take care of her teeth at all costs. It wasn't like she could pop into the future every six months for a checkup.

Curious, she asked, "Would you ever want to travel east? Move back?"

"No." There was no question in his voice. "My life is here."

She liked his certainty. He knew where he belonged, what he'd do with his life, and she respected that. So many people in modern times flitted from one thing to the next, never knowing what they should do or where they should go.

There was a sense of peace in knowing those things and never questioning them. That was something she wanted for herself. "It must be nice to know where you belong."

"Everyone has a place they belong."

She shook her head. "I'm not so sure of that."

"You belong here, or else you wouldn't be here."

Did she? If she belonged here, then why hadn't she been born during this time? It'd taken fairytale-like powers to bring her here. "I hope so."

"I'm sure you'll feel better about things once you find your fiancé."

She wished she could turn around and look at him right then. His voice sounded hard as if he didn't like thinking of her with another man. Could he possibly be jealous?

"Why did you decide to become a mail-order bride?" he asked, then quickly added, "Forgive me, it's none of my business."

"No, it's all right." She wasn't truly a mail-order bride, but she could still answer his question. "I came because there was nothing for me in my old life except my father. I love him dearly, but I wanted more. I want love, home, a family of my own."

"And you couldn't find that back East?" He sounded doubtful.

"No." She laughed. "Pathetic, isn't it?" She dared a look behind her, and he looked at her intently before she twisted back around to the front.

"I find it hard to believe you weren't fiercely sought after. A woman like you would have suitors at her door day and night."

Her heart beat faster, unable to believe what he was saying. Did he really think she was worth all that? "There were a few, but none of them interested me." The guys who'd wanted to date her weren't exactly winners. They spent their time either drinking and partying or playing video games in their mothers' basement.

He was silent for a moment. "Your fiancé must be an excellent man then."

She didn't want to lie to him again, so she remained silent. A moment later, she cleared her throat. "You're sure your mother won't mind me staying with her?"

He laughed. "No. I have a feeling the two of you will get along just fine. My father died soon after they arrived. My mother did whatever she had to do to protect our future."

"She sounds like an amazing woman."

"She is."

The way he spoke about his mother touched her heart. She could tell he truly loved her, appreciated her, and respected her. Although he was a grown man, it was obvious he still took care of his mother.

The differences between him and the men back home were staggering. As she learned about him, she couldn't help but feel admiration for him.

He had to be the right one for her. She could just feel it. Perhaps she should just tell him everything now. "I think—"

"The house is just over the hill," he said, speaking at the same time. "Forgive me. What were you saying?"

She was about to tell him who she really was, but just then they crested the hill, and he stopped his horse. The air left her lungs in a rush. "That's your mother's house?"

"Yes. Well, technically it's mine, but she lives with me."

She stared dumbly at the mansion in the valley below. The structure was sprawling even by modern standards. Even the stable was larger than most midsize homes. "This is yours?" she asked, trying to take it all in.

"It is. I would've told you before, but I didn't want you to think I intended anything untoward. If it would make you more comfortable, I can sleep in the barracks with the other men and leave the house to my mother and you."

"Absolutely not. I'm not going to kick you out of your bed."

He laughed. "No. We have several guest rooms, so that won't be a problem."

She closed her eyes, berating herself. She hadn't even thought that she might *actually* be taking the bed he slept in. Heat swept through her just thinking of it.

What was she supposed to do now? She'd thought he was only a simple man, one working on someone else's land—

She spun toward him. "The river? Does it belong to you?"

He looked at her seriously but then nodded.

"And all the land we rode over? Is it all yours?"

"It is."

She felt sick and turned back around, her dreams crashing around her. He couldn't possibly be the man for her then. This man, Logan Walburn, was a man of means. His destiny was already written out, and she wouldn't interfere with that.

Besides, he could have anyone. Why would he want someone like her? Someone who had to leave her own home in the future to travel back in time for something she didn't have?

She wanted someone simple. Someone who had nothing, someone she could build something with. That man wasn't Logan. He already had everything.

And she had nothing to offer him.

He urged the horse forward, leaving her shattered dreams behind them.

CHAPTER 4

I f there was somewhere to hide, Gemma would. Even from this distance she could see the bustling activity at the house. Everyone would soon know about her. There'd be no getting away from it.

But before they got any closer, he slowed his mount again, stopping completely and dismounting.

Frowning, she looked down at him. "Is something wrong?"

His eyes trailed over her denim shirt and jeans. "No. But I thought you might be more comfortable changing before we approached the house."

She nodded immediately. "Yes! Yes, I think that's a good idea. Thank you." The last thing she wanted to do was make a spectacle of herself. And dressed as she was, it was guaranteed.

She swung her leg over the saddle, but before she could jump down, he stepped forward, hands around her waist again, and brought her down slowly.

As before, her heart beat quicker, but she squashed that feeling. This man wasn't for her, and basking in her attraction wouldn't help anything. She moved out of his reach, gripping her bag. "So I'll just..." She glanced around until she spotted a large tree. "I guess I'll go change behind that?"

Was that completely inappropriate? She wasn't sure what other option there was.

He nodded briskly. "That should be fine. No one's out here, and I'll turn my back."

"All right." She didn't waste another moment debating it and headed for the tree.

She didn't question whether he would peek or not. She already knew he was a man of honor. She could've changed right behind him, and he probably wouldn't have glanced back.

She didn't know if she would've been as strong.

She raced around the trunk, squatting down to riffle through her bag. She pulled out her wrinkled dress, shaking it a few times in hopes of fixing it, but there was no use.

It was a mess, but it would have to do.

She stripped out of her shirt and pants, folding them quickly before donning the dress. She should probably wear a corset, but she couldn't stand the thought of it, and besides, she hadn't been able to find something accurate for this time. Hopefully, it wouldn't be difficult to pick one up.

She packed everything once she was dressed and smoothed her skirts before stepping out from behind the tree. "All set," she said, feeling like she was dressed up for Halloween.

He turned around to face her, then froze, glancing the length of her dress.

When he didn't speak, she shifted from foot to foot. "Is something the matter?"

He approached her slowly, still looking at the dress. "This is yours?"

"Yes." Panicked, she wondered if she'd sewed something

wrong. Was she off in her styles for this time period? "Is something the matter?"

"No. I just wouldn't have guessed."

She frowned. "Guess what?"

He gestured to the draping, pleated skirt. "That you'd have something so fine."

Glancing down at her dress, she realized she'd made a mistake. "Oh! Well, my other dresses weren't nearly as fine. I brought this to be my wedding dress," she quickly said, hoping it would explain the modern quality.

His features cleared. "I see. That makes more sense. It was smart of you to keep it close. It would've been a shame to lose such an elaborate garment."

She pasted a smile on her face. "I agree. I'll have to see about purchasing more appropriate gowns."

He frowned again. "Depending on your fiancé's income, gowns like this might be appropriate for day-to-day wear."

She shook her head. "I don't think so. I don't remember who he is, but I know my intended isn't a man of means."

He looked as if he wanted to say something more but decided against it. Instead, he held out his hand for her. "Come, let's ride the rest of the way to the house and get you settled."

She took his hand, and he guided her to the horse, lifting her gently and setting her sideways to accommodate the dress. He climbed behind her, only gently holding her around the waist.

He was being delicate, clearly overthinking how he treated her and touched her. Had the gown really made that much of a difference? Somehow, he seemed even more guarded now, as if the dress had changed something between them.

He didn't say anything else as they rode to the house.

Workers called out greetings to them, and Logan acknowledged each of them by name.

Stopping in front of the house, he dismounted and helped her down quickly without lingering. "If you'll just follow me, we'll get you settled."

He barely looked at her. What was happening here? Why would a dress make such a difference?

He led her up the steps to a large wraparound porch. The furnishings out here were wicker with lush cushions. But as she stepped into the entry, her breath whooshed out. Rich, gleaming paneling lined the walls and the grand staircase. Light filtered into the room in an array of colors from the large stained-glass window by the stairs.

It smelled of lemon, apples and cinnamon, and freshly cut flowers. It was more than she ever imagined a home could be, and it was even grander than she'd anticipated from the outside.

Whoever Logan Walburn was, his mine must have produced insane amounts of gold to be able to afford a lifestyle like this.

She planned on striking her own claim and building a house later on. But something at this level had never entered her mind. The cost in modern times was staggering, and she couldn't even fathom what it would take to build one here.

If she had any other lingering ideas about Logan being the one for her, they were now crushed. Logan was destined to marry an heiress or some other grand lady. That certainly wasn't her.

"Logan, I thought I heard you come in. You're home earlier than I expected."

Gemma turned toward the staircase and saw an older woman descending. That must be his mother...except she didn't quite look like she belonged in a house like this.

Her dress looked nice, but it was plain, and Gemma could

see the material had been turned out a few times. Was Logan stingy with his money? But if he was, why had he offered to buy her things before taking her to her fake fiancé?

"I found someone while riding." He placed his hand on her lower back and brought her forward. "Mother, I'd like to introduce you to Miss Gemma Watts. Miss Watts is a victim of a stagecoach robbery."

Her light-brown eyebrows rose. "You're lucky to be alive. Most times, all the passengers are killed."

Gemma cleared her throat. "I jumped." That was sort of true—she'd jumped through time anyway.

"How long have you been on your own?"

"It's hard to say." She shifted on her feet. She didn't want to lie any more than she had too.

Logan cleared his throat. "I offered to let her stay here for a few days until I can take her to town and find her fiancé."

His mother looked at her curiously. "Are you a mail-order bride?"

"Yes."

"I'm sure your fiancé is very concerned. Especially if you've been missing for a few days. You are more than welcome to stay here, but are you certain you don't want to head into town immediately?"

When Gemma didn't respond, Logan spoke for her. "She hadn't much contact with him, and the letters they exchanged were with her belongings. She doesn't remember his name."

"Oh dear." She looked at Gemma sympathetically. "I can understand how distressing that must be."

"It is. Thank you for allowing me to stay."

Logan smiled at his mother. "I think you're going to end up having a lot in common."

"Is that so?" his mother asked, glancing at Gemma's ornate dress.

He laughed. "Mother, I found her in pants panning for gold in the river."

Gemma's eyes bugged out. "I didn't think you'd tell her that!" Then, realizing she'd scolded him, and in front of his mother no less, she looked at the older woman, horrified. "I apologize—"

The woman laughed and waved her hand. "Oh no. Please don't apologize. My son is right. I do like you. The fancy dress threw me off, but I can see you're not the type I thought you were."

Gemma knew it was a compliment, and her shoulders relaxed. "You're right." She grabbed a fistful of skirt. "This is beautiful, but it's not me." Her voice lowered. "And it's *so* uncomfortable."

His mother laughed, and even Logan chuckled—even though saying such a thing was completely outrageous in this time period.

His mother walked over to her and looped her arm through Gemma's. "I think we're going to become friends rather quickly, don't you?"

"Yes."

She started leading Gemma toward the stairs. "And you lost all your belongings?"

Before Gemma answered, she looked over her shoulder at Logan. His eyes lingered on hers, and she saw longing there. Desire.

It was the same emotion she felt running through her veins.

But no matter how much she was attracted to him, no matter how much she respected him or appreciated his mother, she wouldn't see him again once she left here in a few days. With any luck, he'd be out of the house most of the time she was here, seeing to the mine and property.

Because she worried she might change her mind if she spent any more time with him.

⁂

LOGAN'S MOTHER LED GEMMA INTO A BEDROOM WORTHY of a princess. "This will be your room."

She walked in, trying not to gape and failing miserably.

She smiled. "I'm glad you like it."

"It's the most beautiful room I've ever seen." It looked just like a museum she'd been to, with an elaborately carved bedroom set and canopied bed. "Thank you, Mrs. Walburn."

"Please, call me, Alison."

Gemma looked around, feeling uncomfortable. "I'm not certain that's proper."

"*Hang* proper. I think you'll enjoy your time here, Miss Watts. The rules are much less strict, and there's freedom for women like us." She bobbed her head. "You might not be able to ride through town in your breeches, but if you want to ride through the fields here, no one will bat an eye." A glimmer entered her eyes. "I've trained the workers well in that regard."

Gemma guffawed. "I'm glad to hear I might be allowed some liberties. If I have to wear dresses like this every moment. I might go mad."

Alison cocked her head. "Did your family allow you to dress as a man often? Is that why you aren't used to it?"

This was slippery ground. "Yes. My mother abandoned my father and I when I was young. I didn't have much of a woman's influence growing up."

"Ah. That makes a lot of sense." Gemma appreciated the woman's lack of pity. "A man doesn't quite know what to do with a daughter on his own."

"You've just described my father perfectly." She laughed, feeling wistful as she thought of her childhood.

"You miss him, don't you?"

"I do. And he's going to miss me as well."

"Can he not travel west?"

Gemma shook her head. "No. He has a successful business in New York. He can't leave."

Alison shrugged. "People move and start over all the time. You never know what might happen."

"That's true." Gemma didn't know what the future held, but she knew she'd never see her father again.

It pained her to think of it.

She straightened her spine, deciding to push forward with her plan. "Mrs. Walburn—Alison," she corrected herself at the woman's look, "I don't know who my fiancé is, and unless I'm certain of him, I can't get married."

"Of course not! And once words spreads of what's happened to you, there will be men who'll try to trick you into marriage."

She hadn't even thought of that. "Why on earth would they do something like that?"

"Because there's not enough women. You must have realized that. Why do you think men send out for brides like you?"

Gemma was being an idiot. Of course, she knew that. "I know. I'm sorry. I'm just so disoriented." She held a hand to her head. "What I was saying was that I need to find something to do if I can't find my intended. I want to provide for myself."

Alison nodded firmly. "We will find you a position. In fact, there will be a job open here if you ever want it."

The generous offer stunned her. "How kind. I'm not certain what I would do, but I'm willing to learn, and I'll work hard."

The woman smiled. "I know you will. I can tell that about you. You're like me, willing to work and earn your own way." She shook her head and chuckled. "I wish I could have seen my son's face when he caught you in the river."

Gemma's lips twitched. "He thought I was a boy."

Alison hooted and slapped her knee. "Bet he was surprised." Her eyes twinkled. "You know, it was in that exact river that I found gold. It was the start of all of this." She gestured to the house. "He's heard the story plenty of times, so it must've been like seeing history. I'm sure it shocked him."

Gemma could only imagine.

Alison patted Gemma's arm. "Rest now, and I'll have a tray brought up. We can talk more tomorrow, maybe come up with a few ideas for jobs if you think it truly might be an issue."

"Thank you." Gemma couldn't stop saying it. She was so grateful she'd come here and found the Walburns. She'd thought she'd prepared enough, but if anyone else had found her, things could have been a lot worse. "I'll see you tomorrow."

Alison walked out of the room after a final goodbye and closed the door.

Gemma flopped onto the bed. This was all like some elaborate dream. She just wished she knew if it would end up being a good dream or a bad one.

CHAPTER 5

C ursing floated into the house through the open
windows, and Logan's feet slowed. He cocked an ear,
listening to the feminine voice and grinned. That wasn't his
mother or one of their maids.

That was Gemma.

He really shouldn't like that about her, but he couldn't
help himself.

Gemma was unlike every lady of his acquaintance—and
he loved it.

Why did she have to be engaged already? Fate was so
cruel.

He changed direction and headed toward the back door
before he could stop himself. He should stay away from her,
but right then, he didn't care.

He needed to know why she was cursing.

As he stepped through the doorway, everything became
clear. She was wearing the fine dress she'd worn the day
before, but she was hunched over the wash basin, attempting
to scrub her denim pants—*attempting* because she splashed
water in waves onto her fancy getup while the washboard

wobbled around, constantly shifting before she could get a good scrub.

She cursed, repositioned the board and tried again, concentrating so hard her nose scrunched. When it moved again, she laid the pants over the side and threw her hands up. "I don't get this! It seriously can't be this hard."

She glared at the wash bin, and he laughed.

Her head shot up, her eyes connecting with him before they narrowed. "Do you find this funny, Mr. Walburn? Because it's not. I'm ready to murder it."

"Should I call the sheriff?" he asked, his tone serious. "He doesn't take kindly to murder."

"It might be worth it," she muttered. "I can't get this to work."

"That's because you're doing it all wrong."

Her hip popped out as she crossed her arms. "Oh yeah? Why don't you come show me how it's done."

"Gladly." He pushed off the house and strode toward her. "The reason it's moving around so much is because you haven't secured it. If you do this"—he showed her how to anchor it—"it'll be a lot easier." He picked up her pants. "Then take the garment and the soap like this, rub them together, and then start scrubbing on the board." He demonstrated each step, moving with easy familiarity.

She blew a tendril of hair from her eyes. "Why do you know how to do that? Isn't it women's work?"

He laughed. "My mother doesn't believe in men's work and women's work. To her, it's just work and every able body better know how to do it. She had me doing the laundry from a young age, and then, even after we got help, she made me do it on occasion just to keep me humble."

Her lips twitched. "I like your mother."

He chuckled. That didn't surprise him in the least. "She likes you too."

"I'm glad. You know, I wanted to thank you again for helping me instead of shooting me."

"It could've gone either way."

She narrowed her eyes playfully. "You would have shot me in the back?"

"Of course not," he scoffed. "I would have shot you in the front."

A devilish glint entered her eyes, and by the time he realized what she going to do, it was too late.

Scooping handfuls of water, she splashed him with sudsy water. Sudsy, *freezing* water.

He jumped back, sucking in a breath. "What was that for?"

She shrugged, but he noticed her smile before she looked away. "Oh, I don't know. You just looked like you needed to cool off a bit."

"Is that so?" Two could play this game. He stepped closer to the bin. "You know, doing laundry is hard work. You look a little warm too."

Her eyes widened. "You wouldn't dare!"

"I wouldn't bet on that." He reached into the water, expecting her to dart out of reach.

But instead, she shrieked and leaped for the bin, splashing him again before he had a chance to attack.

Shocked, he hesitated a moment, allowing her to splash him several more times before he cupped his own handfuls of water.

The first attack hit her shoulder, and she squealed but didn't let up her assault.

Laughing, he splashed her again as they circled the bin, trying to get away from each other while still remaining within range of the water.

Once they were both completely drenched, she giggled and stepped away with her hands held high. "I surrender."

"Never surrender." Pouncing, he wrapped his arms around her and pulled her in tight. He'd just intended to capture her before she could splash him again, but once their wet clothes met, the heat of her body seeped through to his skin, and all laughter died on his lips.

He stared into her hazel eyes, the colors taunting him with secrets. Who was this woman? Where had she come from?

Why can't she be mine?

He'd never wanted anything more in his life than to kiss her, to grip her hair in his hands, and sink into her taste.

Her fingers inched up his chest, and her tongue darted out quickly to wet her lips, almost bringing him to his knees. "Logan..."

His closed his eyes, praying for strength, but couldn't let her go. He squeezed her tighter against him, the wet clothes almost no barrier to her body.

He craved her with a frenzied need.

But no matter how much his body wanted to take over, his brain reasserted itself.

He released her, but she didn't scramble away like she ought. "Why?" she asked softly.

Looking into her eyes, he didn't try to pretend to not understand. "Because you belong to another."

Her mouth opened, but then she shut it.

Bitterness swept through him. She couldn't deny it either. It didn't matter how much he desired her or how she might feel about him. She'd made promises to another. And honoring them had to come before everything.

With a deep breath, he gripped her shoulders and stepped away, knowing his control was hanging by a thread. "I can take you into town tomorrow if you're ready. It's probably best if you find your fiancé as soon as possible."

Mutely, she nodded. "All right."

He glanced at the basin. "And we can have your clothes washed. You needn't trouble yourself."

"I think it's something I'm going to have to learn anyway. I don't know if my husband will have anyone helping us."

He gritted his teeth. Gemma deserved to be taken care of. It was obvious she was capable, but he still wanted to do it, to make sure she never doubted how special she was.

But that might not happen. She could be marrying anyone. A wealthy man or one of the poorest miners. He had no idea.

And neither did she.

He looked away from her. "I'll take you first thing in the morning."

"I'll be ready."

He walked back into the house, unable to say anything more without begging her to stay.

⚜

THE RIDE TO TOWN WAS FILLED WITH AWKWARD SILENCES and stilted communication. Gemma wished they'd chosen to take two horses instead of the carriage—even if the likelihood of her falling off was high.

That had to be better than this.

She didn't know why Logan was so hot and cold with her. She could tell he wanted her, but then he'd shut down.

She didn't understand why it would matter if she had a man waiting. He knew she didn't love her fictitious fiancé, and she wasn't married yet. Surely, people broke off their engagements in this time too.

Perhaps it wasn't that common? Gemma thought she'd known everything she'd need to know, but the longer she was here, the more she realized how truly wrong she was.

This ride was only one example of that.

The landscape was breathtaking, rugged, and wild, with the cleanest air she'd ever breathed. She wanted to bask in it, to celebrate it, but she didn't think Logan would appreciate it.

Still, when would things ever be this easy again? He might not know it, but there wasn't a fiancé waiting for her, and soon, she'd have to figure out how to survive without Logan's generosity.

She didn't want things to end poorly between them. Even if they weren't meant to be together, couldn't they at least be friends?

She inhaled a deep breath, blowing it out slowly. "I don't think I'll ever get sick of the air here. I've never breathed anything like it before."

"I imagine New York would be much different," he agreed.

"More than you know." She was just thinking of what it was like with millions of people crammed into such a tiny space. The thousands of cars, the pollution, the crime. It truly was an entirely different world.

But even in this time, New York was completely different than here. The air quality had to be even worse, poverty afflicted most of the population, and hunger and disease were rampant. "I know it must have been hard growing up, but you're lucky to be here."

He nodded once, not arguing the point. But he didn't say anything else.

She leaned against her seat and held her face up to the sky, enjoying the warm sun's rays on her skin. "I stayed up far too late last night, looking out my window."

Even though he didn't want to talk, she could tell she'd intrigued him. He glanced over at her for the first time. "What were you looking at?"

"The stars." She opened her eyes as if she could still see

them. "You can hardly see them in New York with all the lights."

"It's hard to imagine a sky without them."

"You don't notice after a while. And life gets busy. When does a person have time to stop and just look at them? Like, really look at them?" Gemma certainly hadn't. And she regretted it.

In the few days since she'd arrived, she'd noticed the change in pace. Things were slower here. There weren't cars to take you places, or phones to call a friend just because you were thinking of them. TVs, computers, texting—none even existed.

And without them, how did people spend their time?

It'd been a difficult adjustment. After she'd fallen in the river, she'd been so consumed with trying to survive and finding gold that she hadn't really noticed. But here at Logan's house, all her needs were provided for. She had nothing to fill her time.

She needed to work to not go insane.

"I can't remember the last time I did that," he admitted. "Just lie in the grass and watch the stars. There's always something that needs to be done, something that needs my attention."

She glanced over at him, wondering what his daily life was like. Did he really work himself that hard? Did he need to?

She'd heard more and more about the Walburn Claim. It was massive. They could've moved back East and had one of the finest homes money could buy. But they'd remained here, working day in and day out. "I think it's something you have to make time for."

And even though she'd guarded her heart from him, her shield was starting to crack, and the desire to make him slow down, to show him that life could be even more, filled her.

It didn't matter how many times she told herself she couldn't have him, she didn't care. She still wanted him.

And part of her was starting not to care that she might be screwing up history or that he deserved more than she could give. Wasn't love the most valuable prize of all?

"We're coming up on Main Street."

At his announcement, she sat up on the bench to get an unobstructed view of her new home. Houses appeared more frequently until they were next door to each other, each as tidy and well-kept as the next.

"You'll be able to find almost anything you need here. The town is still small, but it's growing rapidly."

She couldn't look away from the cute storefronts. "Why is that? Are people finding more gold?"

She saw him shrug out of the corner of her eye. "There's always more gold here. But no. It's mainly because of the Copper Kings."

Her head whipped around, recognizing the name. "The Copper Kings? They're here?"

He looked at her curiously. "Yes. Their mine opened not long ago. Do you know of them?"

She didn't know much, but she'd come across plenty of research about them. They'd been—were—powerful, rich men who'd run one of the largest copper mines in the world. There'd been problems, and mining wasn't exactly safe, but the wealth that mine produced had shocked the world even then—now. *Ugh.* Time travel was confusing. "Yes. I think I've heard of them before. I just had no idea the mine was here."

He nodded but turned his attention back to the compacted dirt road. "They've brought in more workers, services, and shops than ever before. They even helped build the new school, church, and medical clinic. One of them is the doctor there."

"Fascinating." To her, this was all history, but it was unfolding before her eyes.

He looked at her curiously again but didn't say anything. He pointed out several places she might find of interest. "The bank, the mercantile, and Sally's café. We also very recently got a new bakery where you can get simple fare. If you're looking for something more elegant, you'll find it at the Winthrop Hotel."

Her mouth hung open. "There's a Winthrop Hotel here?"

Amused, he pointed out the structure. "Yes. It's not as grand as the ones in other cities, but Winthrop runs it himself with his wife, Willow."

It took all of her willpower not to let her jaw hang open. She'd been in the Winthrop Hotel in New York. She'd never been able to afford a night there, but just being inside had been an experience. Their hotels were some of the most lux, exclusive hotels in the world.

And they had one in this little town. "I would love to meet them."

She couldn't help herself. She loved romance novels from this time, but the history had fascinated her as well. She had an almost overwhelming urge to know who the people really were. Perhaps she could write it all down and bury it somewhere for someone in the future to find.

"I can arrange it if you'd like. We're associates."

Warily, she glanced at him again. Logically, she knew he was wealthy beyond imagining, but that wasn't what she thought of when she was around him.

In fact, those things just melted away, leaving Logan, the man. But real life wasn't that simple. "Thank you."

He pulled up in front of the mercantile. "I know my mother offered you several of her dresses, and you've said you didn't need anything else, but why don't you have a look around and just double-check?" He parked, jumped out of the wagon, and came to her side. "Let me help you down."

He reached up for her, and this time, she was ready for the shock of his touch. But instead of lingering as he sometimes did, he released her immediately.

She really shouldn't be disappointed. "Thank you."

He nodded once. "Would you like me to join you?" The offer was polite, but she knew he wanted to excuse himself.

"No. I'll be fine on my own."

"All right. But if there are any problems, scream and I'll come for you."

The thought was so ludicrous all she could do was nod. "I will."

She stepped onto the boardwalk, and a feminine voice sounded behind her. "Mr. Walburn? I didn't know you'd be in town today."

The syrupy sweet voice had Gemma turning back toward Logan and the woman who was now plastered to his side.

"It's nice to see you again, Miss Pollard."

The woman's laugh tinkled in the air, making Gemma want to vomit. Who was she?

"I've told you to call me Eliza." The blonde woman trailed her fingers up Logan's chest in a teasing way.

Gemma wanted to stomp over and flick her hand away from him. Instead, she tilted her chin up. "Mr. Walburn?" Gemma raised her voice slightly to get his attention.

His focus immediately returned to her. "Yes, Miss Watts?"

"I've decided I might need assistance after all." She hated saying it but knew it would get the other woman away from him.

Eliza glared at her from under her lashes, but when Logan looked at her, the sugary sweet expression took over again. "Why, Mr. Walburn, I don't believe I've met your new friend. Who is she?"

Gemma stepped off the boardwalk. "She," she said before Logan could answer for her, "is Miss Gemma Watts, and she is in need of her escort."

Eliza pouted and looked at Logan as if she hadn't heard anything Gemma said.

He sighed. "Miss Watts was the unfortunate victim of a stagecoach robbery. My mother has taken her in for the time being."

"Oh dear!" Eliza's gasp was so over-the-top she could have won the lead in her old high school's play. "It's so like your generous mother to take her in."

"Yes." He didn't say anything more.

"Taking on a charity case only makes me admire her more."

Gemma had dealt with her share of mean girls in school, but none of them could hold a candle to this chick. "I'm sorry, who are you?" Gemma finally asked, done with the entire conversation.

Eliza's smile turned condescending. "I'm Miss Eliza Pollard. Mr. Walburn has been courting me the last few months."

Gemma gasped, completely unprepared for that bit of information. Logan was courting this horrible woman who was the meanest, rudest person Gemma had ever met?

Seeing she'd hit her target, Eliza looped her hand through Logan's arm. "I hope you'll tell your mother I'm looking forward to the dinner party tomorrow night. I haven't been to your home in ages."

He said something that Gemma couldn't hear. "Dinner party?" Why hadn't Gemma heard of it?

"Yes." Eliza cooed. "Mrs. Walburn hosts the most exquisite parties with only the most exclusive guests." Her eyes trailed up and down Gemma's dirty dress, an eyebrow raising once she saw the inch of mud staining her hem. "I wouldn't worry too much about it."

It took everything Gemma had not to unleash her tongue. There were so many things she could say, so many things she could do. But what would any of it accomplish?

Logan had already decided this woman was worth his time. He wouldn't be courting her otherwise. And if that was the type of woman he was interested in, there was no way someone like Gemma could make him happy.

She could never be like Eliza, could never put anyone down or make them feel less. She'd never spend her days primping and preening or going to exclusive parties. Honestly, it sounded like the most wretched life she could imagine.

But instead of saying any of that, she notched her chin up. "You're right. Such things aren't worth my notice." She looked at Logan. "I'm afraid I was wrong. I don't require your assistance after all." She spun on her heel and walked into the mercantile, not once glancing behind her.

CHAPTER 6

Confused, Logan watched Gemma walk into the mercantile. What had just happened? One minute she'd been fine, then the next she'd stormed off.

Was it because of Miss Pollard?

The woman in question was still making cooing sounds and holding onto his arm. It took all of his patience to allow her to remain hanging onto him when all he wanted was to shake her off and be rid of her.

He'd only courted her for his mother's sake, but he wished more than anything to break ties with her completely.

All her nonsense about his mother nauseated him.

If his mother knew the things Miss Pollard said, she'd probably throw a fit as well. The most sought-after people? Like any of that mattered to his mother.

She held those dinners for one purpose and one purpose only: to further the mine's business. That was it. He could barely get his mother to purchase appropriate clothing let alone host large society parties. She had zero tolerance for fluff and preening.

Why she insisted he court the ladies in town when they

were all like this confounded him. She couldn't possibly want him to marry any of them, could she?

"I want to say again that I'm so impressed by you and your mother's generosity. Taking in a stranger?" She gave him a doe-eyed look. "Such kindness. I'm not sure how many others would take such a risk."

He frowned. "What risk is there? She's a lone woman."

She shrugged daintily and looked at the storefront. "She could have an ulterior motive. To steal from you perhaps? You can never be too careful."

He disentangled himself from her and faced her. "Miss Watts was a victim of a terrible crime. She came out west to become a mail-order bride. She knows no one, has no family here, and all of her worldly possessions have been taken. I think everyone should show a little kindness."

Realizing she'd made a mistake, she nodded her head enthusiastically. "Oh my goodness! I had no idea. The poor thing." She looked back toward the mercantile with sympathy, but Logan wasn't buying any of it.

But instead of arguing, he only nodded.

"But who is her fiancé? If she came here to marry someone, why isn't he here taking care of her? Why are you seeing to her needs?" Her face still looked sympathetic, but he could hear the malice in her words.

He gritted his teeth. "She lost his letters and can't recall his name since they hadn't corresponded much. That's why we're here today. I'm sure whoever sent for her has been looking for her."

"Of course! I'll do everything I can to help. I'm sure we'll find her groom before long."

He didn't miss her smile before she left to begin her search. A part of him wanted to call her back, to tell her she'd misunderstood and there was no one waiting for Gemma.

But it was the truth. Someone *was* waiting for her. Someone had sent for her and was waiting to marry her.

And now, with Miss Pollard looking for them, Logan knew it was only a matter of time before the man in question was found.

He wasn't naïve. He knew he was a catch for the single women in town. They wanted his wealth and his land. And he was young and handsome enough that their lives would be easy. But he deserved so much more than that. And they did too.

Why marry if not for love?

He sighed, looking toward the mercantile once more. Unfortunately, not everyone felt the same.

He wanted to go into the shop, to beg Gemma not to marry her fiancé. But he wouldn't do that. Instead, he turned down the street, heading for the hotel. Surely someone would know something about who was waiting for Gemma.

And the sooner he handed her over, the sooner he'd be able to move on as well.

GEMMA STAYED INSIDE THE MERCANTILE FOR HALF AN hour, pumping herself up enough to walk out of the store and possibly see Eliza again.

Oh, Gemma understood exactly what had happened out there. Eliza had clearly already staked Logan for herself and was defending her claim.

It had infuriated Gemma to see her next to Logan, acting as though they were so close and would only become more so.

How could he court someone like that? Everything she thought she knew about him had to be reevaluated. How could the person she was coming to care for want someone like that? It wasn't possible.

But none of that should matter anyway. She'd already determined he wasn't right for her. Why should she care if he courted someone terrible? It shouldn't affect her at all.

But looking at the situation logically didn't help. She was jealous. There was no getting around it. But what could she do about it? What did she *want* to do about it?

She needed fresh air to clear her mind and reevaluate what she wanted in her life.

She waved to the shop owner and walked out the door, taking a deep breath. No matter what else was happening, she had to remember that she'd chosen to come here and find the love of her life.

That person wasn't Logan. So even if she was jealous, she had to get over it. Move on. Decide what she wanted to do and move toward that goal. The right man would show up at the right time, she was sure of it.

"Miss Watts! You're alive!"

Startled, Gemma stopped at the edge of the boardwalk as a man ran and fell to his knees in front of her. He grabbed her hand, placing a wet kiss on the back of it as he looked up at her adoringly. "Darling, I had so despaired! I thought you'd been murdered."

Everyone around them had stopped and were watching them. "Um." She tried to pull her hand away, but the man wouldn't let her go. "I beg your pardon, but I don't know you."

His face fell, then he jumped to his feet. "But, darling, you must. It's me, Robert Blaine, your fiancé."

"My *what*?" Her voice rose. "No that's not possible. You are certainly *not* my fiancé."

He looked at her tenderly. "I was told you didn't remember my name. Perhaps you hit your head once you fought off the Indians and jumped from the racing carriage."

"After I what?" She held up her hands, warding him off. "Oh no. No, no, no."

He took her hand again before she could pull it out of his reach. "Yes! I heard all about your ordeal. It's no wonder you can't remember. Let us marry now. I'll take you home and care for you until you remember everything."

He started tugging her down the boardwalk before she got her wits about her and dug in her heels. "Where are we going?"

"To the church."

"I am not marrying you!"

He didn't release her. "Of course you are. I'm your fiancé. I've already explained everything."

She was so astounded by his arrogance she couldn't even scream for help. She tried to talk sense into him for another moment before she jerked her arm away. "I don't know you!"

Another man raced over to them, pushing Mr. Blaine out of the way. "Step away from her!"

Relief rushed through her. "Thank you, sir. There's been a misunderstanding."

He tossed her a reassuring look before facing the man. "Don't ever presume to touch my fiancée again, Robert. You won't like what happens."

She choked. "*Your* fiancée?"

"Sweetheart, I'll explain later," he said, not even glancing back at her.

She'd had enough. "Don't *sweetheart* me! I'm not your sweetheart."

She took a few steps backward, watching to make sure the men wouldn't follow her, and ran into something hard. Hands reached out to steady her. "Woah there, Miss Watts."

Gasping, she twirled around, looking into the handsome face of another stranger. "Pardon me. I was trying—"

"To get away from these imbeciles. I knew you'd be smart. Just like in the letters we exchanged."

"You've got to be joking!" she screeched, moving past him down the boardwalk and ignoring the men calling out to her.

At the mercantile, she was met with another group of men pleading with her to hear them out.

They converged on her, and her back met the wall of the building. "Step back, please."

They were all speaking at once, reaching out and stroking her arm or trying to take her hand as they all swore to have her letters, to love her.

But none of them were listening to her.

She knew there weren't many women in town, but they'd never get anyone to agree to marry them if they behaved this way.

She stepped away from the wall, her hands balling into fists at her side. "I said get back!"

At her yell, the men's declarations of love ceased, and she glared at them and the other men who flocked to her from down the street. "I want you all to hear me and understand well," she said, her voice carrying. "I am not marrying any of you! Not today and not ever. If you think a woman wants to be accosted in the street, you sure are wrong about that. I might not remember who my fiancé is, but I guarantee he wouldn't behave like this. And if he did? The wedding would be off!"

She nodded once at the end of her speech, grateful she'd seemed to get through to them. But after another few seconds of silence, the men continued on as if she hadn't spoken.

One voice rose above the crowd. "I believe the lady has already spoken."

Relief coursed through her as Logan stepped through the

crowd, asserting himself in front of her so she was pressed to his back.

"As she said, she's not marrying any of you. And if you think to harass her again, you'll have to go through me."

"This doesn't concern you, Logan! You can't keep my fiancée from me. I have rights!"

Sweat broke out beneath her dress as she realized one wrong move could cause a riot. How was Logan going to stop them from taking her if that's what they really wanted?

"Until Miss Watts finds her true fiancé, she's under my protection. She is not to be harassed, cornered, or even spoken to unless it's with her consent. If I hear of anyone doing something like this again, I'll ruin you."

Several of the men grumbled, but then, as if realizing it wasn't worth it, the crowd dispersed.

Logan stood as he was, guarding her and warding away the few stragglers who looked as though they wanted to approach her again. But eventually even they must have realized it was futile and left as well.

When Logan's muscles finally relaxed, she sagged against him. She'd almost been taken against her will. The shock of it wove through her.

She'd known it was dangerous coming here, but she hadn't imagined anything like that happening.

He turned and looked at her, quickly wrapping his arm around her. "Follow me."

He led her between the buildings toward the back, stopping at a shallow nook where no one would be able to see them from the street.

She stood close to the building as he shielded her from anyone who might've followed. "Are you all right?" he asked.

"Yes—I don't know." She was shaking. She knew the danger had passed, that everything was okay now, but she couldn't stop the reaction. "Those men—"

"Will never harm you. I'll protect you."

She shook her head, not looking at him. "You won't always be there. At some point, I'll be alone again."

He leaned a hand against the building, using his other to tip her chin up so she'd look him in the eye. "I swear to you, Gemma, no one will touch you without your permission, no one will ever corner you like they did today."

He was breathing heavily, and she could see the promise in his eyes. He would protect her no matter what the cost.

But why did he care so much? "You can't promise that. What if you marry soon? Your wife won't want you looking after another single woman." She shook her head, thinking of Eliza. "Don't make promises you won't be able to keep."

He leaned in even closer. "I swear to you. Nothing will stop me from protecting you, from coming for you. Never doubt it."

Her heart beat hard against her chest. He was promising her more than anyone ever had in her life. And right then, she didn't care that he was wealthy, that he was courting Eliza. None of it mattered except that he was here and was saying things to her she'd only ever heard in her dreams. "Logan—"

And before she could say anything more, his lips were on hers. She didn't know if she'd reached up for him or if he'd come to her, but the moment they met, an explosion rocked within her heart.

Never had she felt so out of control and settled at the same time. Never had she felt this kind of burning passion, this need to be connected with someone until they were one heart.

She pulled at him, wanting him closer, wanting more. She wrapped her arms around his neck, delving into his thick, light-brown hair.

It was like a trigger for him, and he became more aggressive, kissing her until her toes curled.

This was what she'd always wanted. This was what she'd dreamed of, why she'd come to the past.

He nipped her lips, and she opened for him, tasting him as deeply as he tasted her.

He brought his hands up to hold her, one at her waist and one at the side of her neck. Changing the angle, he slowed the kiss until she felt each lick and pull all the way to her toes.

The feelings coursing through her were too much, too overwhelming. Her eyes watered. This was right. It had to be.

She wanted to tell him everything.

She murmured his name, and as if it were a bucket of cold water, he sprung away from her.

Stunned, all she could do was gape at him. "Logan?"

She moved forward, reaching out for him, but he held up his hand. "We can't do this."

The four words shattered her heart. "Why?"

"Because you're taken. You've made promises."

She wanted to blurt out that she'd lied, that no one was waiting for her. But what would he say? Honor was important to him, and she'd deceived him. "But I don't remember to whom. And how am I ever to know if one of the men out there claiming I'm theirs is actually telling the truth?" She took a deep breath. "And there's one more thing."

She waited until he looked at her. "What?"

"I don't love him. I don't care about him. I care about *you*."

He shook his head, already denying her words. "I took advantage of you here. You were shaken by what happened. I should've never done that."

She crossed her arms. "What do you think I am, Logan? A damsel in distress? I'm a *woman*. A fully capable, intelligent woman. I made the choice to kiss you just now. I'm not some bystander you accosted with your lips. I want this." She took a step toward him. "I want you. Don't ever say I don't know what I'm doing."

He raked a hand through his hair, looking everywhere but at her.

Then dread pooled in her belly. Did he regret it because he had feelings for another? Had he already made promises to Eliza?

Mortification swept through her. "You know what? Let's just forget this ever happened. It's clear you wish it never had. I appreciate your offer of protection, but I'll be just fine on my own." If she had to start carrying a gun, she would. "I think we've seen enough for today. No man is here waiting for me."

She spun on her heel and walked back to the wagon. She couldn't get home soon enough—

Except, she realized...Logan's ranch would never be her home.

CHAPTER 7

The moment they returned from their disastrous trip to town, Gemma was certain of one thing—it was time to move on. She couldn't stay in town, with how the men had reacted. It would never be safe. And she was finished with wanting Logan.

She'd been right this whole time. He wasn't for her, and she'd been a fool to forget that for even a moment.

She walked in the house and headed straight for Alison. As agreed, Gemma was hired to work in the house.

It wasn't ideal—she wasn't really suited for anything they needed done—but it was a start. She would work at Logan's estate, get her feet under her, and then move on. She was strong and young, and she would learn.

She just wished she'd realized this was how it was all going to turn out before she'd come. If there was a way to go back to her time... But that wasn't an option now, and it did no good for her to dwell on the past.

She'd finally figured out how to do laundry, so that's what she did first. She'd been working since sunrise, and her hands and forearms were red with irritation from the caustic soap.

But she'd done it.

She'd washed everything she'd been given and was doing it well. She needed to dust next and then polish the entry, but compared to laundry, that almost seemed like a vacation.

She was armed with cleaning supplies and had already completed half of the room when a knock sounded at the door. She looked around, unsure if she should answer it or not. Who was in charge of that?

Finally, when the second knock sounded, she put down her rag, rubbed her hands on the work apron she wore over one of Alison's older work dresses and answered the door—to her nightmare.

"Miss Watts, is that you?" Eliza Pollard asked, trying to sound unsure, but Gemma could see the gleam in the vicious woman's eyes.

"It is. If you'd like to step into the parlor, I can let Mrs. Walburn know you're here."

The woman stepped into the house like she already owned it, her lilac gown exquisitely bedecked in bows and ruffles. She waved her hand. "Oh, I'm not here to see Mrs. Walburn. I'm here to see Logan—Mr. Walburn," she stressed as if she'd accidentally slipped and used his first name.

Gemma grabbed a handful of her skirt, worried she'd pummel the snotty girl. "Then please make yourself comfortable, and I'll have someone fetch him for you."

She turned to leave, but Eliza called out, "Be a dear and bring tea. I have a feeling I'll be here for some time. Oh, and tell the cook not to send any of those jam cookies from last time." She scoffed. "Honestly, with how much money they have, they should fire the cook and get a new one."

Gemma was done. She didn't curtsy, didn't say anything more, she just left. If Logan and Alison wanted to fire her over it, she didn't care. She might be working for them, but she wasn't a servant, and she refused to be treated like dirt.

She knocked on Logan's door, her heart racing knowing she would see him in a moment, but she pushed the feeling down.

"Enter."

She opened the door softly. "Miss Pollard is here to see you."

Surprise lit his eyes. "Gemma, what is this?" He jumped out of his chair, gesturing to her dress as he came to her. "Why are you wearing that?"

She swallowed hard. She'd assumed his mother had told him about her new position, but apparently, she hadn't. "I'm no longer a guest here, Mr. Walburn. I've been hired as staff for the house."

He was shaking his head before she even finished speaking. "No."

"It's true. I spoke with your mother after we got home yesterday. I'll be working in this position until I find my groom, or I decide otherwise."

He stepped closer to her, but she moved out of range. "Gemma, you don't have to do this. You can just stay with us as a guest. You don't need to work."

She looked at him, at the confusion on his face. She wasn't doing this to hurt him. "I do need to do this. You saw what it was like in town. It'll always be like that."

"Your real fiancé will have proof. He'll have your letters."

"But what if he doesn't? What if they got lost or he got rid of them?" She knew there was no one waiting for her, but she still couldn't bring herself to tell him the truth. "What if he changed his mind?"

But before she turned away, he blocked her exit. "What do you mean?"

She looked him in the eyes. "What if it was all a hoax? Someone writing letters for sport. What if no one ever comes for me?"

He shook his head. "That's not possible. He's out there, and he wants you."

"You don't know that."

His jaw clenched, but he remained silent.

She shook her head and ducked under his arm. The whole conversation was pointless. "Your guest is waiting. I'll bring her the tea service she requested—"

"Gemma—"

"Mr. Walburn." She curtsied, but it wasn't in a subservient way. It was a dismissal, and they both knew it.

She couldn't run from the room fast enough.

❧

GEMMA TRUDGED TO HER BEDROOM, EXHAUSTED FROM A long day. She'd spent hours polishing silver and setting an elaborate table for Alison's party tonight—the one Eliza had gushed about.

It was everything the viper had said and more.

And even though Gemma was bone tired, her heart was even more weary. She didn't belong at that table. She was poor, had no family.

She was nothing.

Alison had tried to get her to come tonight, but that would be a mistake. She would only be an embarrassment to the family, and she refused to be a spectacle.

Almost as if she'd imagined her, Alison appeared in her doorway. "Everything looks perfect, Gemma. You might not have known how to do laundry or milk a cow, but you sure know how to set a table."

She smiled half-heartedly. "I've had a bit more practice with this one."

"Have you decided what you'll wear tonight?"

Gemma sighed. "I already told you I'm not coming."

"This isn't up for debate," Alison announced. "You're coming to the dinner."

"I don't even have anything appropriate to wear. Besides, I'm a servant."

Alison pursed her lips. "We both know you're no servant. You might be earning your keep, but you're too terrible at your chores to have been doing them your whole life."

Gemma's mouth dropped open.

"Oh, don't act all shocked. It doesn't matter to me one way or another. But I'm telling you now, Gemma, you'll be at this party. Even if I have to pull you by your ear."

Gemma didn't doubt the woman would do it. She threw her hands in the air. "Fine. I'll be there. But if you're humiliated by what I wear, it's your own fault."

Alison smiled with satisfaction. "I thought you might say that." She looked down the hall and crooked her finger.

"What are you doing?"

"Oh, just having something delivered." The housekeeper who'd been kindly showing Gemma how to perform her chores stepped in and laid one of Alison's exquisite silk gowns on the bed. "We're a similar size."

Gemma reached over and gently touched the material. She'd never seen anything so fine—in either time. "It's beautiful." She longed to wear it. "But I can't."

Alison scoffed. "Of course you can. And you will."

Before Gemma could say anything else, Alison left, closing the door behind her and leaving Gemma to look at the gown.

She couldn't really wear it, could she? Perhaps the better question was *should* she? This wasn't her life. At least, it wasn't long term. If she ever made enough to afford a luxury like this, it would be years—possibly decades—away.

She ran a finger over the material again, wishing.

What could one night hurt though? And it wasn't like

Alison had given her a choice. This was the last time she'd be able to do something like this, to be elegant and attend a fancy party.

Before she realized she'd even made the choice, she reached for the dress.

Tonight, she'd be Cinderella.

CHAPTER 8

Logan hated these affairs. It was a chance for people to enter their home, pretend they were more important than everyone else, and gorge themselves at his expense.

He agreed with his mother that they were necessary, but that didn't mean he had to like it.

He greeted his guests as they entered the parlor. The men wore formal black suits while the women wore silks and lace in every color. Jewels sparkled around their necks, but none of it impressed Logan.

"Winthrop." He greeted the hotel owner, genuinely happy to see him, then turned to his wife. "Mrs. Winthrop, always a pleasure."

Her blonde hair was swooped back in a style as elaborate as her skirts. "I thought I've told you to call me Willow."

Logan grinned. "So you have."

Her eyes lit with amusement. "You still won't though, will you?"

"Perhaps someday, Mrs. Winthrop."

Rhys Winthrop had married well, as had several of Logan's other friends.

In gold-rush towns like these, there were all sorts of people—good and bad. Rhys was one of the good ones. "I was grateful that both you and the McDermotts accepted our invitation this evening," he said, speaking of Rhys' sister and her husband, one of the Copper Kings. "I haven't seen them in some time."

"The copper mine has been taking up a lot of their time," Rhys said.

"Ah." Logan wasn't surprised. It was one of the largest in the world. "I'm glad to hear that business is going so well."

Rhys gave an amused smile. "No one's complaining, that's for sure."

Logan laughed, movement catching his eye.

Rhys glanced behind him. "Looks like you have more guests. We'll talk later."

"Thank you." He said his goodbyes then looked to the next group, and his enjoyment dropped.

He held out his hand to the older man. "Mr. Pollard, it's lovely to see you." Unable to put it off, Logan nodded to Mrs. Pollard and Eliza. "And your family. It's lovely to see you Mrs. Pollard, Miss Pollard."

Eliza preened, and the urge to excuse himself almost prevailed over his good manners.

"You're too kind, Mr. Walburn," Eliza said, offering him her gloved hand.

He couldn't refuse it without a scene. He placed a quick, light kiss on the back of her hand, and then spoke to all three. "Enjoy yourselves this evening."

After the three trailed away, his mother stepped up to his side and whispered, "How is Miss Pollard doing this evening?"

"She seems well, Mother."

She looked at him knowingly. "You know, I only wanted

you to start courting someone. It doesn't have to be her if you're not interested."

He shrugged. To him, one woman was the same as another in that regard—except Gemma. "It doesn't matter to me. I was doing it to please you."

She eyed him as if trying to figure something out. "You know, if you were interested in someone else, someone who works hard but has little to her name, I would approve."

He shook his head, shutting her down. "That can never happen."

"I wouldn't say *never*. Things happen all the time." She held up her hands. "But I won't push it if you don't wish me too."

"She's promised to another," he said, knowing he should remain silent. But hearing his mother's approval only made things worse.

She waved to one of their guests then leaned toward him. "But not married."

She made it sound so simple. But it wasn't. Things were complicated.

"I can see you're still debating over it, so I won't say anything more. However, I think you should prepare yourself. You might be surprised this evening." And before he could ask her what she meant, she moved away, joining another conversation.

He wondered what she was up to but figured he would find out eventually. He greeted several more guests until pale blue silk caught his eye from down the hall—opposite from the front door.

Staring at the ruffled, draped skirt, his gaze made its way up to a tiny, cinched waist and lace bodice. When he finally made it to the woman's face, his breath escaped him. "Gemma." He was at a loss for words. "You're breathtaking."

She glided toward him, blushing, but he couldn't stop

looking at her. He'd been insanely attracted to her in denim clothes and even the work dresses she'd donned the last few days, but how she looked now, he'd never forget.

Her hair was curled and pinned up with large ringlets escaping. She didn't have any other embellishments such as the dripping diamonds and sapphires some of the others wore, but he couldn't imagine her looking any more stunning. Those stones would only take away from her true beauty. "I hardly know what to say."

Her lips curved. "I look presentable, then?"

"More than. You're the most beautiful woman I've ever seen," he said honestly.

Her mouth formed an *o*, but she didn't say anything. He knew he shouldn't have admitted to it, but Gemma needed to know her value. He refused to have her mingle with the other guests without knowing her worth.

He took her gloved hand in his, bringing it to his lips and brushing it with a soft, lingering kiss. He wanted to say more, do more, but with so many other people around, he restrained himself. "I'm glad you came tonight."

Her lips quirked. "Your mother wouldn't let me sit this one out."

He snorted. "That sounds like her." He offered his arm. "Let me escort you in."

"Don't you have more guests you need to greet?"

"None that matter."

She ducked her head a moment but then looked up. "All right." She tucked her arm in his and smiled.

It felt so right it made him stagger. He'd only known her for a short while, but she had completely changed his life. Everything he thought and felt was different. He wanted things he'd never dreamed of before.

Home. Family. Love.

Those things used to fill him with dread. They'd always

been a burden, a duty he'd have to perform one day. But with Gemma next to him, starting a family was no longer a bleak prospect. He looked forward to it.

He introduced her to his friends and associates, not letting her go for even a moment. He didn't care how it might appear to others.

A few moments later, dinner was announced.

He probably should have escorted his mother, but when he glanced at her, she only looked at him approvingly. If Gemma was embarrassed by the attention he gave her, she hid it well. In fact, she seemed somewhat oblivious to it. And that pleased him.

He brought her to her seat, somewhat frustrated she was several places away from him. He wouldn't be able to talk with her during the meal, but it was probably better that way.

As each day passed without a man showing up to claim her, his reasons for staying away faded. All he'd been able to think about was their kiss, how she felt in his arms—and how he could do it again.

Once the guests were seated, he stood, holding his glass for a toast. "I'm grateful to see so many good friends here tonight. Promise Creek is our town, our legacy. Each person in this room has seen to its prosperity. Through our work and connections, I know it will only continue to grow into a place we can be proud of—into a place our children will be proud of. To Promise Creek."

Everyone echoed the toast and drank, and the first course was brought out.

He conversed with the people around him, wishing he'd been seated by more agreeable people. But this was business. Mr. Pollard commented on the expanded mining operations in the area, but Logan only responded with passing comments as he watched Gemma. She chatted amiably with the people around her, charming everyone. She was a natural in this situation, and it pleased him to see that she could make conversation as easily with one of the neighboring mine owners as she could the pastor.

Mr. Pollard followed his gaze and then frowned. "I see we have a new guest tonight. My daughter mentioned she's one of your maids. Is that true?"

Logan didn't like the man's tone. "She is helping around the ranch currently, but her circumstances are very unusual."

"I don't understand what possessed you to invite her tonight. It isn't done." The man shook his head as if truly baffled, and Logan's blood began to boil. "If my daughter is ever in charge here, I guarantee such things will stop."

That was enough. "Whoever I marry would never bar anyone I deem worthy. And although you might question my choices, I hope in the future you'd have enough sense to keep them to yourself. Miss Watts is an honored guest here no matter what she might do for work."

Mr. Pollard's face grew mottled. And when Logan was finished, he looked out at the rest of the table, realizing everyone had heard his impassioned reply.

Gemma was looking down at the table as if ashamed.

"I want everyone here tonight to know one thing. I don't care how much money you all have. Most of us started with nothing. And I hope that we can work together to make this town into a place that is a haven for all. But to do that, we need to stop this pretentious nonsense. Everyone starts somewhere. It doesn't make them any less worthy of our respect. And if anyone in this room is insistent upon such things, they're free to leave. Such things will not be tolerated."

He glared around the room as if daring someone to stand and leave. He knew he was making a scene, drawing a line in the sand that might make enemies, but he didn't care. Some things were worth standing up for.

After an awkward silence, Lucas McDermott spoke up. "Many of you know that I came from nothing. I worked in the lowest positions and made a pittance. People looked down on me, they thought me beneath them, but they were wrong. We are all equals no matter what we do. And if people insist on living in the past, the future will crumble." He held up his cup and toasted Gemma. "You're welcome here, Miss Watts. We're in this together."

As everyone murmured their agreement, Gemma leaned back into her chair. She seemed uncomfortable with the attention. "Thank you. This is all very new to me. But I appreciate your support, and I appreciate your inclusion."

A few more people toasted her words, and then the conversation moved on. After the next course, Gemma excused herself. The urge to follow her was strong, but unless he wanted to completely reveal his heart to the entire room, there was no way he could leave. He just hoped she was all right.

GEMMA DIDN'T KNOW WHAT TO THINK OR FEEL. ALL SHE knew was that she needed to escape. She might not be a historian, but she knew that people weren't treated equally here. Your status depended on how much you had and what kind of jobs you held—not so completely different from modern times.

Weren't doctors and lawyers more desirable, at least by societal standards, than trash collectors? Those professions had status, wealth. Divisions were even more extreme during this time period, and women had no standing whatsoever.

She'd known all that before coming, but actually living through it was a completely different experience. How would she tolerate such things, knowing how different it could be?

As impassioned as Logan's speech was, she knew not everyone in that room agreed with him. Some would never accept her. Some would always look down on her. And it wouldn't matter if she made her own fortune or married into one.

In their eyes, she had nothing, not even family connections. And that made her nothing.

She paced in the library, knowing she'd have to return before anyone came looking for her, but she just didn't know if she could.

She took a deep breath then blew it out slowly.

They might look down on her, but she needed to remember one thing—she wasn't the person they all thought she was. She was a modern woman, educated, and had traveled through time to be here. How many people could say such a thing?

She was amazing and talented—maybe not at laundry—but she'd owned a business and could cook. She had skills that she could share with the people here. She needed to stop reacting to everything and be intentional in what she did.

She could thrive here. She *would* thrive.

It was all up to her.

Feeling more settled, she walked to the door, only to have it open before she reached it. "Oh, pardon me. I was just..." But anything else she had to say died on her lips. "Miss Pollard? What are you doing here?"

The blonde, petite woman waltzed into the room as if she owned the place. "I wondered where you ran off to. I thought it was time to have a little woman-to-woman talk."

Gemma knew exactly what Eliza wanted to say. "Right. You want me to stay away from Logan. He's yours. Whatever." She rolled her eyes and moved to walk past her, but Eliza's hand shot out to stop her.

Eliza's eyes narrowed, and she glared at Gemma. "I don't

think you understand, but you are correct about one thing. He *is* mine. This home will be mine. Everything you've been touching with your low-class, dirty hands, is mine. You might be staying here, you might be getting cozy with Logan and his mother, but know that they'll tire of you. You don't have what it takes to hold his attention for long. You're only a novelty to him."

Gemma couldn't deny anything Eliza had said. But she was wrong about one thing. "I might be low-class, but my hands are clean. I haven't needed to scheme my way into Logan's life or heart. I'm here because they want me here, and as long as they do, I'll be here."

Eliza shook her head. "You really don't want to get in my way. I guarantee you won't like what happens."

Gemma sighed, pushing Eliza's hand away. "Honey, you don't know who you're dealing with either."

Finished with the conversation, Gemma walked out of the room, but instead of heading back to the dining room, she headed for the back stairs.

She wasn't running away. But she refused to sit and play nice. She was exhausted from a long day, worn out from the drama, and just wanted to get in bed.

"Gemma!"

Her foot was on the bottom stair when Logan caught up with her. She closed her eyes in a brief prayer.

"Gemma, where are you going? You can't be retiring already."

She turned to face him. "Yes, I can. I'm going to my room, I'm getting in bed, and I'm going to sleep like the dead."

Worry filled his eyes. "Don't let what was said in there bother you. I don't care about them. I don't care what they think. Anyone who actually matters isn't part of the stuck-up, pretend aristocracy like the Pollards."

Hearing him refer to Eliza made something in her snap.

JANELLE DANIELS

"If you don't like people like that, then why are you courting her?"

His jaw hardened. "It's complicated."

She shook her head and laughed bitterly. "Actually, it's not. You court someone you're interested in marrying. If you weren't considering her as a potential wife, then you wouldn't be doing that."

She spun away to head upstairs, but he caught her wrist, bringing her back to face him. "I don't care about Eliza. I never have. I've only courted her because it pleased my mother. Never me. She's not anything like the woman I want."

For the first time, she embraced the jealousy raging through her. None of this was fair. "And who is that? Some other wealthy woman who will bring you more land and money?" She rubbed her head, hating herself for even asking. She didn't want to know who he really cared for. All she wanted to do was escape. "Let me go."

But instead of letting her go, he jerked her forward until she landed against him. She looked up at his face, meeting his wild eyes. "You want to know who I want? *You*, Gemma. You. I've held back, tried to be the better man, but it's so difficult every time I see you. I know you belong to someone else. I know it isn't right to take you for myself, but I can't think of anything else. I'm starved for you. I'm crazed for you. And I know I'll never want another but you."

She couldn't breathe. "You don't know what you're saying."

He cradled her head in his hands. "I know exactly what I'm saying." And then his lips crushed down against hers.

All she could do was feel. The light swirled around her in a rainbow of color as sensations wove through her. She felt disoriented, out of focus—the only thing clear was him.

She moaned, opening for him. Her mouth, her mind, her heart.

He was everything she wanted, everything she'd hoped for.

And she took the leap into love.

She didn't know how things would work out, she didn't know if he'd been fated for another, but, for now, he was hers.

She kissed him back wildly. Using her body and her lips to tell him the things she wasn't ready to say. She wanted him, needed him, just as much as he needed her.

The kiss gentled, slowed, until he leaned his forehead against hers. "Was that clear enough?"

A chuckle escaped her, even as she tried to get back her breath. "Yes."

He nuzzled her lips, kissing just once more before stepping back. He looked at her and then slowly grinned.

She reached up to her hair. "What is it?"

"You look beautiful."

She laughed. "I probably look a mess."

Heat entered his eyes. "A thoroughly kissed mess."

His words and his look sent butterflies through her. "I should head upstairs."

"Will you return?"

She had fully intended on going to bed and forgetting the whole night. But with what had just happened between them, she wanted to be near him. "I'll just fix my hair and be back down in a bit."

"Good. Hurry." There was promise in his eyes.

She picked up her skirt and ran up the stairs, his laughter trailing behind her.

CHAPTER 9

Logan put aside all the work he could and set off for town. He had one goal: to find who Gemma was engaged to and end it. What had happened between them last night had changed things.

He wanted her, and he wanted all ties she had with another man severed.

Then he could propose to her.

They'd start their life together, and it would be unlike anything he'd ever imagined before. He wanted to sit and talk with her for hours, to know where she'd come from, who her family was. He wanted to know how she wore her hair when she slept, if she preferred to eat breakfast in bed or in the dining room. He wanted to know every detail about her that made her who she was.

He wouldn't pretend he was ignorant of what it all meant. He was in love with her and wanted to spend his life with her.

And if she wasn't in love yet, he knew she was well on her way. He couldn't be the only one who felt this.

He just had to find the nameless, faceless man first.

As he rode into town, he greeted several people who

called out to him. He normally would stop and chat with each of them, but he didn't have time today. He needed help, and he knew exactly the men he should talk to.

He stopped his horse in front of the Copper Kings' office in town and dismounted, quickly securing his horse before walking into the building.

A woman with tumbling, fiery red curls looked up from her desk. A smile crossed her lips as she rose. "Mr. Walburn, it's wonderful to see you."

He tipped his hat. "You as well, Mrs. Eversley."

"What can I do for you?"

He looked around the office. "I was hoping to catch one of the Copper Kings. Your husband, Chase, or Lucas, ideally."

She shook her head regretfully. "They're both at the mine today. They should be back in a few hours if you'd like to stop by again, or I could take a message for you."

"That isn't necessary. I was just hoping to ask if they've heard of someone. One of their workers, perhaps."

She looked at him curiously. "I don't know everyone, but I might be able to help you. Who is it you're looking for?"

"I don't know his name."

That didn't seem to deter her. "A description then? I've met several of the miners."

He sighed. "This probably sounds insane, but I don't know that either."

Her eyebrows lifted over her expressive, moss-colored eyes. "I'm sorry." She laughed. "But you'll have to give me something to work off of."

He shook his head in amusement. "I have a woman staying with my mother and I. Her stagecoach was robbed on its way here. She came as a mail-order bride."

Her expression fell. "That's terrible! Is she well?"

"She is," he hurried to assure her. "She wasn't injured. But the problem is that her belongings were stolen, including the letters she'd exchanged with her intended. They hadn't conversed long, and she can't remember his name."

"That shouldn't be a problem." She frowned. "The man must be waiting for her."

He nodded slowly. "That's what we thought as well, but once word spread, everyone was claiming to be her fiancé. It was chaos."

Her eyes widened. "My goodness. I can just imagine."

"I was hoping you'd know of a man who's talked about sending for a bride."

Her eyes narrowed as she thought. "No. I haven't. However, that might be because the news hasn't gotten to me. Chase might know." She rolled her eyes. "He always knows all the gossip."

He snorted in amusement. "I can see that about him."

"I can ask him and Lucas when they return. I'm sure if it was one of the workers, they would've heard about it. I'll have word sent to you if they know anything."

That was the best he could hope for. "I appreciate your help."

"Of course." She walked him to the door but stopped him before he could walk out. "The woman, will she remain at your house?"

"She will."

Understanding lit in her eyes. "I see." She chuckled. "Well, I was going to offer her a place to stay if she was in a rough spot, but it sounds like she's taken care of."

He nodded once. Now that he intended to marry her, it might not be proper for her to stay with him, but he wasn't going to let her go. "She's well taken care of."

"I can see that. Please let her know that if she ever needs anything—whether its advice or just to spend time with other women who understand what it's like to be uprooted—have her pay me or any of the other women a visit. We're always excited to welcome another woman into town."

He could just picture Gemma settling into her new life here. "I'll let her know. Thank you." He tipped his hat one last time and stepped out the door, feeling a little lighter.

But as the day progressed and he spoke with Rhys Winthrop, the blacksmith, and several other men who might have heard about a mail-order bride, he became more frustrated.

No one had heard of a bride coming. It was like she'd come from nowhere. But that wasn't possible.

People didn't just appear from thin air.

⚜

GEMMA WAS HUMMING AS SHE SWEPT THE FLOOR IN THE sunroom, feeling like everything was right in the world. Officially, nothing had happened between her and Logan, but it felt like everything had changed.

It was amazing how a person could go from despair to happiness in only a matter of minutes. But that's what it was like.

Although she'd felt Eliza's daggers for the rest of the night, Gemma hadn't cared. She only had eyes for Logan. And it had been apparent to everyone else in the room that he felt the same.

Everything she'd done, everything she'd sacrificed had been worth it.

Her broom slowed.

All she needed to do was tell him who she really was. He'd believe her, wouldn't he?

She resumed her sweeping, faster than before. He had to believe her. It was the truth, after all. She'd have to also tell him that she'd lied about being a mail-order bride, but he'd understand that as well.

She hoped.

"Gemma?"

Just hearing his voice sent goosebumps racing over her skin. She looked over her shoulder and grinned. "I was wondering when you'd get home. It must've been a long day." She put her broom aside and walked to him before pulling him into a hug.

He froze at the gesture, and she realized people probably didn't do such things here. They weren't even engaged, after all.

She squeezed him one more time before easing back. "I apologize. I'm rather affectionate."

She was slipping her arms from him when he grabbed her wrists, tugging them back around his neck. He wrapped his arms around her waist, holding her close. "I like when you touch me. You have my permission to do so whenever you want."

Her heart quickened. "Promise?"

"Absolutely."

"Good. Because I enjoy it."

"I do too."

It was easy between them, so good. She couldn't wait to get married and have even more together. "Were you at the mine today?" she asked. He frowned, and she realized something was wrong. "What is it?"

"I was in town, looking for your fiancé."

She froze. "Oh."

"I couldn't locate him. I went everywhere, asked anyone I thought might have heard something. It seems as though no one was expecting your arrival."

"I see." She stepped away from him, needing space for

this conversation. She took a deep breath before turning back to him. He remained quiet, watching her.

She cleared her throat, gathering her courage. "You couldn't find my fiancé because there never was one."

His eyebrows pinched. "You never had a fiancé? How is that possible if you came as a mail-order..." Knowledge flashed in his eyes. "You lied? You were never a mail-order bride?"

She saw the confusion in his eyes, the hurt. She bit her lip and shook her head. "I can explain."

His jaw hardened. "Was your stagecoach robbed?"

She winced. "No."

He spun away from her, pacing the room. Finally, he stopped and looked at her. "Why lie to me? What is it you're after?" His nostrils flared. "The money? The mother lode?"

"What?" She gasped. "No! Of course not! How could you even think that?"

"I don't know, Gemma—is that even your name?" He looked at her as if she were a bug under a microscope.

"Yes! My name is Gemma Watts. I'm from New York, and I came here to find my husband, even if he wasn't the mail-order groom I told you about."

Pain and anger crossed his face, and he stepped up to her again. "There's another man?" His voice was deadly, and she realized what he was thinking.

She held up her hands, resting her palms on his chest. She expected him to push her away, but he remained still, as if frozen in place. "No. Please, let me explain."

"Speak."

She didn't appreciate the command, but she understood she'd pushed him to the very edge of what he could handle. "It might be a little hard to believe, but I swear it's the truth." Her mouth went dry, words temporarily failing her.

"Go on."

She couldn't look at him, so she looked at his neck. "I came from New York, but not the one you know. I'm from the future."

He inhaled sharply, and she dared a glance at his face. His eyes were narrowed, and she could tell he didn't believe her.

"I know it sounds insane."

"Completely."

"But it's the truth! I'm from the future. The twenty-first century. That's why you found me at the river. That's why my clothes looked so strange."

"If that's true, how did you get here? Did one of the Greek gods send you or something?" he asked mockingly.

"What? *No.*" She was losing him. She could see it. "No. Nothing like that. I was a part of this book club. We read romance novels—romantic tales. There was a woman who came—apparently, she's a fairy godmother—and she told us she could send us to where our true love was, to the man we were meant to find. I'd always loved reading about this time, about men like you who worked hard, settled this territory, and made a life for themselves."

"So, you targeted me. Thought to trick me into marrying you."

"No! Aren't you listening to me at all? I said she sent me to the man I was meant to be with. I didn't know who it was. I had no idea what he'd be like. I wasn't even sure I'd meet him right away. That's how I ended up in the river. When I appeared in your time, I was dropped right into it. I didn't know who you were before we met that day. I hadn't ever heard about you or your claim. I hadn't studied this area extensively."

He still looked skeptical. "So you didn't know about anything here?"

"Well, a few things," she admitted. He raised a brow. "I'd heard of the Copper Kings and had studied them in school.

The copper mine will be so much larger than they realize now. The mine isn't just going to make them rich, it's going to completely throw them into the realm of kings."

He shook his head and turned away from her. "I just can't believe this, Gemma. Everything is so farfetched. Traveling through time? It's the stuff of fairytales."

She went to him and placed her hand on his back. She wanted to beg him to look at her, to believe her, but he would have to come around to accepting this on his own. "I know. At first, I couldn't believe it either, but when other girls from my group started disappearing, I knew it had to be true."

"They all were sent here?" He looked as though he'd caught her in another lie. "I haven't seen any other new women."

She shook her head. "No. They went all over. Some went to medieval Scotland, others to Regency England. We were sent all over the place, to wherever we were meant to go."

His jaw clenched. "I need proof. I'm sorry, Gemma. It's too much to take in."

She nodded quickly. "I understand completely. If our situations were reversed, I'd feel the same way. But I'm telling you the truth, and I can prove it."

"How?"

"Remember my bag? I didn't want you to carry it for me because it had my things from the future. I brought medicine and technology, and other things I thought I would need to survive here. I knew if anyone saw it, they wouldn't understand. They'd think it was witchcraft. But it's not. I have a device. It's a cell phone that fits in my hand, and it lets me call anyone anywhere in the world in a few seconds."

He shook his head. "Impossible."

She grinned. "It true. We can't call during this time because the rest of the technology isn't set up, but I brought it because it can also take photographs and videos—sort of like moving pictures but much better quality."

His jaw went slack. "Show me."

She took his hand and squeezed. "Follow me."

He was starting to believe her! She was thrilled he was taking it so well. In a moment, he'd see the pictures, know she was telling the truth, and everything would be all right. "I have everything in my bag in my room."

They walked up the stairs, and he waited in the hall as she entered. She went over to the dresser where she'd stored the pack.

Opening the drawer, she stared dumfounded.

"What's wrong?" he asked.

But she didn't answer. She quickly closed the drawer and opened the one below it. Then the one below that.

Panic enveloped her as she tore open each drawer, finally looking under and behind the piece of furniture.

Realizing something was really wrong, he asked, "Gemma, tell me."

Dread settled in her belly as she faced him. "It's gone. Someone stole my bag."

CHAPTER 10

"What do you mean someone stole your bag?" Logan asked, still reeling from Gemma's story.

She gestured widely, panicking. "I mean I put my bag in this drawer, and it's gone now. Someone moved it."

"You're sure you put it there?"

"Of course! I've had to be very careful with the contents. I didn't want anyone to see them."

Although it wasn't proper, he moved into the room, rechecking each drawer and the other places she'd looked. He also looked through the cupboard by her bed, under her mattress, and under the heavy piece of furniture.

She paced the room, agitated. "I don't know who could have taken it. No one has been coming in here for anything."

"What about to clean?"

"No! I've insisted on doing everything myself for this very reason."

She'd had the pack. He'd seen it with his own eyes. "It couldn't have just disappeared..." Then he thought about how she'd just appeared in his time above the river.

Sensing his thoughts, she glared at him. "The pack

wouldn't have just disappeared. Someone had to have taken it."

"But who? And why?"

She chewed her lip. "I don't know. Not unless they knew what was in it. I made sure to bring something that no one would want, nothing that would attract too much attention."

He agreed no one would steal it for the bag itself. "Then why take it from your drawer?"

"None of this makes sense." She collapsed into an uphol-stered chair.

She looked so dejected. He wanted to go to her, to tell her it would turn up. But this was a little too coincidental. She claimed she was from the future, and the only proof she had was in a bag that had magically disappeared. "When was the last time you saw it?"

"I don't know." She shook her head, concentrating. "I took a picture out the window a few days ago. But I put it away again..." Her eyes widened. "It was in the drawer before the dinner last night. I remember I was getting hose out of another drawer, but I accidentally opened that one, and it was there."

He shook his head. "No one came up here. And besides, why would they take something of yours? What would they gain?"

"I don't know why they wo—" She staggered back. "Eliza. It has to be."

"Eliza Pollard? Why?"

Gemma glared at him. "You were courting her. She expected to marry you. She even warned me to stay away from you."

He frowned. "When?"

"In the library. She came in and confronted me. You found me just as she'd left."

Last night replayed in his mind, and he nodded slowly.

"And then you came back, and it was obvious to everyone that things had changed between us."

"She would have known any chance she had with you was gone. She could have sneaked into my room, found the bag, and then taken it."

It was a stretch, but it was possible. "Why would she do that?"

She gestured wildly. "I don't know. Maybe she was looking for something that could ruin me?" Her face turned ghost white. "And she found it. If she showed it to anyone…"

He didn't know if he believed her or not, but he didn't like seeing her in distress. "It'll be fine. Everything will be all right."

"You don't know that. You haven't seen what I have in there."

He didn't respond. What could he say? He didn't believe time travel was possible. It was such a stretch of the imagination. And although the timing worked for Eliza to have stolen the bag, it seemed too convenient.

She'd been watching him as he thought it over, and her face fell. "You don't believe me."

"No," he said, trying to soften the blow. "Would you?"

She turned away, but not before he saw her eyes water. He never wanted to hurt her. Reaching for her, he tried to take her into his arms, but she went stiff, refusing the gesture. "I know you don't believe me, but I'm telling you the truth. Whoever has my bag will make it known. Then you'll see."

He raked a hand through his hair. He didn't know what to say, how to make this better. No, he didn't believe her, but that didn't mean he loved her any less. And now that she'd told him there wasn't a fiancé waiting for her, there was nothing keeping them apart. "It doesn't matter to me. I still want you."

She shook her head. "It matters to me. This is who I am,

where I come from. If you don't believe this, you'll never believe anything I tell you about my past. How could we be together?" She laughed humorlessly. "How could you be okay marrying a crazy person?"

He hadn't mentioned marriage yet, but the fact that she'd been thinking of it too only made him want her more. "None of it matters."

"Yes, it does!"

His fists opened and closed at his sides. It was obvious there was nothing he could say to mend this. All he could do was give her time, let this all die down, and then move on. "I'll ask the housekeeper if anyone has seen your bag."

She whipped around. "Fine. But it's a waste of time." She marched toward the door.

"Where are you going?"

"I know Eliza has it. And I intend to get it back."

Logan called after her as she fled down the stairs, but she didn't stop.

She's from the future?

He'd never heard of anything so preposterous in his life. He was too stunned by the fact that she didn't have a fiancé to even fully process her claim.

It couldn't be true...could it?

If she'd had her bag and showed him this *cell phone* from the future, would he have believed it, or would he have brushed it off?

He left her room, walking down the hall without thinking of where he was going. All he could see was the hurt on her face. Regardless of where she was from, he'd never wanted to do that. He loved her. He wanted to take care of her.

But how could what she said be true?

"Logan?"

He backed up a step and looked into the library at his mother. "Good morning."

"Morning." She frowned. "Did I hear Gemma leave earlier?"

He sighed. His mother never missed anything. He sunk into one of the upholstered chairs, putting his head in his hands. "Yes."

He heard her sit in the chair next to him. "What happened?"

He didn't know what to say. Should he explain it all? And if he did, would it turn his mother against Gemma? No matter what had happened, he still wanted her. He let out a long breath. "She told me something this morning that is difficult to believe."

"I see." She cocked her head. "Is it something you can share?"

Gemma hadn't said it was confidential, and, since she truly believed it, she would probably say the same to anyone. "She told me that she wasn't really a mail-order bride and hadn't come here on a stagecoach."

"Oh dear. If that's not the truth, then where did she come from?" She frowned. "You found her panning in the river. How had she gotten there? There wasn't a horse, as I recall."

He looked straight ahead. "She said she's from the future. The twenty-first century. She said a woman sent her back here to find the love of her life."

Silence echoed through the room, and he finally glanced at his mother. She had a strange expression on her face. She opened her mouth, closed it, then tilted her head. "And you don't believe her?"

"Would you? It all sounds so insane. How could she have traveled back in time?"

"She had no proof of her claims?"

He shifted in his chair. "She said her bag contains things from the future. Things that are such a stretch of the mind, I

89

can't fathom it. She went to go get it, but the bag is conveniently missing."

She frowned. "Missing?"

"That's what she claims. She said it was here before the party, but now it's gone."

"And she has no idea where it could've gone."

"She suspects Miss Pollard might have taken it."

Understanding lit in his mother's eyes. "I understand. While I'd hate to think the woman capable of such a thing, it is possible. Why didn't you go with her?"

"Because I was still so stunned over her claims." He put his head down. "And I hurt her."

"Because you didn't believe her." His mother quieted. "I know it sounds crazy, Logan, but think about what you know about her. Think about her clothes, about the way she speaks. Have you ever heard anyone talk like that?"

His brows creased. "She speaks a little differently, but she's from the east. It's to be expected."

She shook her head. "*I'm* from the east, dear. The Copper Kings and many of the others are from there as well. Have you ever heard any of them talk like that? Or behave the way she does? There's something different about her. Something more than just being from the east. Think about it, Logan. She's more outspoken, stronger, and more capable than any other woman of my acquaintance. I've never met her equal."

A sinking feeling settled in his gut. His mother was right. What he loved about her was that she was so different than the rest. She didn't care about what other women seemed to waste their time on. She wasn't snippy or looking for a rich husband.

He'd found her trying to make her own way. She wasn't wealthy, yet she didn't know how to do everyday chores.

The more he thought about her, the more plausible her

claim sounded. She *was* different. He'd just been so blinded by his feelings for her that he hadn't seen it.

"If she's from the future, why would she have ever come here?"

His mother's lips slowly curled. "She already told you that. To find the love of her life. And I think she might have found him. Don't you?"

His eyes met hers. "I love her more than anything in the world. I need her with me, and I don't care where she's from."

"I know, dear. And it was obvious to everyone in the room last night as well. Eliza Pollard would have known that." Worry filled her eyes. "But if she's taken Gemma's bag with things from the future, there could be problems."

If everything Gemma said was true—and he believed her now—then anyone who saw those things could cause trouble for her. He jumped from his chair. "I need to get to her."

His mother stood, leaning forward to kiss his cheek. "Go get Gemma and bring her home."

He was still worried about her bag, but a lightness filled his heart. This was where she belonged.

CHAPTER 11

He doesn't believe me.

It was the one thought that kept running through Gemma's head as she rode in the wagon towards town.

She shouldn't be surprised. Her story was completely out there, even in her time. And if someone had told her a year ago that they were from the future, she would have called a mental hospital, no matter what fantastical technology they showed her. She would have thought it was some experimental government stuff. She could've easily rationalized it away.

But even though she knew it would take time for him to come to terms with the truth—if he ever could—it still hurt.

She was in love with him. She wanted to spend the rest of her life with him. But how would that work if he couldn't trust her? Would he question everything she said in the future?

Since she'd arrived in this time, her emotions had been on a roller coaster. Everything she'd planned on, everything she'd expected, had been thrown out the window. None of this was going according to plan.

Maybe coming to the past had been a giant mistake. Sure, she hadn't found love in her time, but she didn't have it here either.

All she had was heartache—and the fear that Eliza would expose her and she'd be burned as a witch.

Did they still do that?

Maybe she should just get her bag and wish really hard to go home. Would that work? Would Dr. Lachele hear her?

After entering town, she'd asked someone for directions to the Pollards' home. Fortunately, they lived in one of the larger homes on Main Street.

She pulled in front of the pristine white house and parked the wagon. The iron fence that surrounded the property was a work of art, and it reminded her of something similar she'd seen on a tour through Virginia City. She wished she could stop and study it, but there wasn't time.

With a deep breath, she marched up the walkway to the front door and knocked briskly.

When an older gentleman opened the door, Gemma smiled. "Good morning. I'm here to see Miss Eliza Pollard."

"Your name, Miss?"

"Gemma Watts."

He opened the door wider, allowing her to enter. "If you'll wait in the parlor, I'll see if Miss Pollard is available."

"Thank you." She walked into the room right off the entry, glancing around at the rich furnishings. Whatever Mr. Pollard did for business, it was obvious he was successful at it. It wasn't anywhere near as grand as Logan's home, but the Pollards were certainly wealthy.

"Miss Watts, what a surprise." Eliza stepped into the room, looking as polished as she had last night.

Gemma turned toward her. "Is it a surprise?"

Eliza smirked. "I don't know what you're talking about."

Gemma sighed. "Look, I know you don't like me. That's

fine. I don't even care. But you know why I'm here, and I'm not leaving without it."

Eliza gave another innocent expression, and fury, hurt, and disappointment rushed through Gemma. "If you want Logan so bad, why don't you just tell him already?"

Eliza guffawed, and Gemma was pleased to see she'd gotten a reaction. "I don't know what you're talking about."

Gemma waved her hand. "Oh please. Stupidity is never attractive. You want Logan. I don't blame you. But if you want him so bad, just go for it. Tell him you want to marry him. Propose even."

Eliza gasped. "A woman would never!"

"Why not?"

"Because it isn't done."

Gemma shrugged. "Maybe not now. But I have a feeling that women are going to have more power in the future. They'll be able to vote, have careers, and even wear pants."

"That will never happen," she scoffed.

Frankly, Gemma didn't care if Eliza believed her or not. People like her only ever cared about themselves. "I'm going to give you a little piece of advice. Although, heaven knows you won't take it. Logan isn't interested in you. I'm sorry. I'm not saying that to be cruel, but to help you so you can move on. You seem like a catch. I'm sure any man in town would be grateful to have you."

Eliza's cheeks pinked with anger. "Yes. Any man *would* be grateful to have me. Including Logan."

"Sorry, hon. He's just not that into you."

"You don't know what you're talking about."

Gemma held up her hands, exhausted. "Look, I really don't care what you decide to do. I only care about one thing. My bag. I want it back."

An innocent expression filled her face. "I don't know anything about your bag."

"Yes, you do. I know you took it. You're the only one who would have. I know you must've been super upset after realizing Logan's preference for me. But I really need that bag back."

Eliza's mouth formed into a firm line. "I'm sorry. I just don't know what you're talking about."

Gemma's eyes narrowed. "I don't think you understand how important that bag is to me. If you don't bring it to me immediately, I'll get the sheriff. And I'd hate for everyone to find out about your part in its disappearance."

Eliza's skin mottled. "You wouldn't dare."

"Oh, yes, I would. Bring me the bag now, and I'll leave quietly. Or I can get the sheriff. You choose."

Eliza glared another minute before spinning on her heel. "Fine. Follow me." She marched out of the room, and Gemma followed her through the home until they entered the library.

Eliza went to the far end, knelt down, and felt along the top of the books on the bottom shelf. A moment later, she removed her hand, Gemma's bag in its grip.

She rose from her crouch. "Here," she said, tossing it over to Gemma as if it were a piece of trash. "Take it. I don't know why you'd want it anyway. There's just hunks of metal."

Relief coursed through her, and she looked through the bag, finding all her belongings. "They might just be hunks of metal, but they're important to me."

She rolled her eyes. "You got what you came for, now leave."

Gemma walked toward the door to the hall and then stopped. "I know you hate me. I probably wouldn't like it if someone came and took the one thing I wanted, either. But please know that there will be someone else for you. Someone perfect."

Eliza lifted her brow. "How touching. Thank you."

Gemma shook her head at Eliza's sarcastic tone and

walked into the hall. Eliza would have a hard life if she continued with that attitude. She'd never be happy, never find love.

She'd be alone—

Someone grabbed her from behind, shoving a cloth over her mouth and nose. She screamed. The noise muffled by the chemical-smelling fabric. She kicked behind her, using all her energy to break free from the unrelenting grasp. But the more she fought, the heavier her muscles became.

As she began to lose consciousness, all she could think of was Logan.

She'd never see him again.

❦

LOGAN FIGURED HE WASN'T THAT FAR BEHIND GEMMA. He'd only spoken with his mother for a bit before grabbing his horse and riding at top speed to the Pollards' home. He would make sure Gemma found her bag, and then he would take her home, where they'd have a long conversation.

He wanted her to know he trusted her, that he believed her. And he wanted to know more about her life and where she'd come from.

He was so lucky to have her. He didn't know who had sent her here, but he was certain of one thing. She was meant for him. No other woman—in any time—was more suited to him.

He wanted a life with her, and, after today, he hoped they would never be parted again.

He stopped his horse in front of the Pollard's home, relieved to see Gemma's wagon was still out front. He knocked on the door and greeted their butler. "I'm here to pick up Miss Watts. Will you show me to her?"

The man frowned. "I'm sorry, Mr. Walburn, but she left a bit ago."

"No. That isn't possible." Logan moved to the side so the butler would have a clear view of the wagon. "Miss Watts rode in that. If she left, the wagon would be gone also."

"Hm. Maybe I was mistaken. Please, come in."

Logan stepped inside and cocked his ear. The place was completely silent. "Where is everyone?"

"I'm not certain. I've been seeing to a task in the kitchen and haven't kept track of the family. If you'll wait in the parlor, I'll look for them."

"I'll wait here." Something felt off.

He bowed his head. "As you wish." He walked toward the back of the house, and a moment later, Miss Pollard came to him.

"Mr. Walburn, is everything all right? I wasn't expecting a visit from you."

She seemed pleased by his appearance, and while he hated to disappoint her, it was time she understood that things were completely over between them. "I'm here to escort Miss Watts home. I assume she received what she came for?" He raised a brow, speaking vaguely in an attempt to minimize her humiliation.

Still, her cheeks colored. "Yes. She got it and left."

Unease swept through him. "She left?"

"Yes. About five minutes ago."

He shook his head. "The wagon is still out front."

"I'm certain she left."

"Did you *see* her leave?"

She pursed her lips. "Well, no. We were in the library, and then she walked out. I stayed inside, so I didn't see her leave."

Something wasn't right here. "Are you certain that's what happened?"

"Yes!" Her eyes widened. "I'm not lying."

He believed her. He looked past her down the hall then glanced to the stairs and into the parlor. There was no sign of her. "She has to be here."

"I'll go see if the servants know anything." She looked uneasy as she went to get answers.

He paced the hall, his heart in turmoil. Something had happened to her, he could feel it.

After a few minutes, when Eliza had returned, saying no one had seen her, his panic escalated. "Gemma! Gemma, are you here?" he yelled, knowing his voice would carry through the house. He didn't care he was acting insane. "Answer me!"

A door opened and closed, and Mr. Pollard hurried out. "Logan, what's going on? Why are you yelling in my house?" He narrowed his eyes disapprovingly. "This behavior is unacceptable."

"I'm sorry, Mr. Pollard. But Miss Watts is missing, and she was last seen in your home."

"I haven't seen her."

"She was visiting with Eliza." The man still looked skeptical. "Her wagon is out front."

"I see. Perhaps she left on foot? She might be walking around town."

It was possible, but unlikely. Gemma wouldn't walk around on her own after her last experience here. "I don't think so."

"I'm sorry, Mr. Walburn, but she isn't here." Mr. Pollard started herding Logan toward the door, but Logan sidestepped him, refusing to be pushed out. "I'm not leaving."

He started down the hall to where he remembered the library was. He'd retrace her steps.

"You'll leave this instant, or I'll call the sheriff!"

Logan looked over his shoulder at the man. Why didn't he want Logan there? Was there something to hide? "Call him, then."

He was turning back around when he saw something dark-green hidden under a hall table. He crouched down and pulled at the bag. His heart slammed in his chest. It was hers. He remembered it from when he'd first found her by the river.

Holding it in his hand, he stood slowly and faced Mr. Pollard. "Where is she?"

The man's face pinched. "Why do you care? She's just a servant. You're lowering yourself by caring for her."

Rage wove through him, but he needed to remain calm if he was going to find her. He took a menacing step forward. "Tell me where she is right now, or I swear I'll destroy you. If you've harmed her, if you've hurt her in any way, you'll pay for it."

Realizing he was caught, Mr. Pollard moved past him to the next door off the hall. He took keys from his pocket and unlocked it. "She'll be fine after she wakes up."

"Wakes up?"

Logan pushed past the older man and into the room, freezing as he saw Gemma's crumpled form on the floor. "Gemma!" He raced to her side, collapsing to his knees.

Fearing the worst, he rolled her over, checking for breathing.

Once he saw her chest rising and falling, he lowered his head in gratitude. She was alive.

"I told you she was unharmed." Mr. Pollard scoffed.

Logan slowly rose to his feet. "This is unharmed? She's unconscious."

He shrugged. "Just a little chloroform. She might have a slight headache once she wakes, but no other effects."

Logan saw red. He launched himself at Mr. Pollard and wrapped his hand around the man's neck, pinning him to the wall.

"Father? Father!" Eliza cried as she ran into the room. She looked at Logan. "Release him at once."

But Logan ignored her. She glanced farther into the room, her eyes widening as she saw Gemma and went to her side. She looked up at her father. "What's happened? Father, did you do this?"

Mr. Pollard remained silent, and Logan squeezed the man's neck threateningly. "Answer her." Logan loosened his grip so her father could breathe.

The older man sucked in a breath, but his expression was belligerent. "Of course I did it, you stupid girl. I had to do something when you failed so miserably to secure your future with Mr. Walburn. Such failure," he spat.

Logan was done listening. "What was your intention? Were you trying to kill Miss Watts?"

"Kill her? No. But I was going to get rid of her." He sounded like it was a small matter.

"How?" Logan growled.

"I knew I couldn't just send her away. She'd only come back. I found a man who was willing to marry her for a price. Once married"—he shrugged—"there was no way you could be with her. She'd be bound to another."

Logan could scarcely believe what he was hearing. "And then what? I would've happily married your daughter?"

"Yes."

Logan reeled in horror. If he'd been any later, Gemma would have been taken from him. "Your plan failed. I'm turning you over to the sheriff."

Panic filled the man's eyes for the first time. "No harm was done. Miss Watts is fine!"

"But she wouldn't have been if I hadn't come for her."

"I didn't attack her. I was protecting my interests."

The man's logic was so twisted that Logan couldn't stand to listen to Mr. Pollard a moment longer. He pulled his fist back and let it fly—landing dead center on the man's temple.

He went slack in Logan's grip, unconscious. Disgusted, Logan let him drop to the floor.

"I'm sorry, Logan. I didn't know." Eliza looked at him with tears in her eyes. "I didn't know he would go that far."

He felt sorry for her. Having a father like that couldn't be easy. "Summon the sheriff."

He expected her to argue, but she only nodded, sniffled, and then left the room to do his bidding. He picked Gemma off the floor, unwilling to let her go for even a moment. He'd take her home so when she woke, she'd know she was safe.

And then he'd never leave her again.

Ten minutes later, Sheriff Morrison entered the room, glancing down at the still unconscious Mr. Pollard then to Gemma. "Is she all right?"

Anger still festered within him, but he nodded. "I got here in time. She'll be fine."

"Miss Pollard told me what her father did. I'll get someone to help me bring him to jail. The judge should be here next week, and he'll see justice done."

Sawyer Morrison had always been one of his friends, and he knew the man was fair.

Logan stood, cradling Gemma in his arms. "I don't believe Miss Pollard had anything to do with it."

"I agree. But she'll be questioned all the same. If I find evidence that she was involved, she'll be sentenced as well."

Logan didn't think it would come to that. "Do you need me for anything else?"

"No. You take care of Miss Watts. I'll handle everything else."

Logan was grateful. "Thank you again."

He held Gemma close to him as he left the house. No one would ever hurt her again.

CHAPTER 12

G emma came to slowly. Her vision was blurred, and she was groggy. What happened? Had someone roofied her drink? She blinked several times until her vision cleared, but she still wasn't sure where she was.

Someone's bed.

She froze then looked over slowly and saw a man sitting in a chair beside her. Then her memories all came back.

She gasped, jerking upright.

The sound woke Logan, and he sprang from the chair. "It's all right. You're safe, Gemma."

Her chest heaved in panic as she glanced around. "What happened? How did I get here?" Her eyes widened. "Someone tried to kill me!"

He sat beside her and pulled her into his lap, cradling her. "You're safe now. Mr. Pollard was arrested and will never harm you again."

His warmth soothed her, calming her more than his words. Finally, she sucked in a deep breath and released it slowly, feeling steadier. "Was he the one who attacked me?" She pulled away slightly so she could see his face.

"Yes. But I found you before he could take you away."

"Away where?"

"He planned to marry you off so I would be forced to marry Eliza."

It was so crazy Gemma didn't know what to say. "He wasn't trying to kill me?"

"No. He drugged you and would have brought you to another man who was willing to marry you."

It would have been horrific, but she was just so relieved she hadn't been near death.

He watched her intently, giving her time to process everything. A million thoughts swirled through her mind as she thought of what might have happened. But all of that faded, and all she could think of was the last few minutes before she'd lost consciousness, the anguish of thinking she'd never see Logan again.

But here he was, holding her in his arms.

She brought her hand up to his cheek, gently rubbing the scruff on his face. He turned his head, pressing a kiss to the center of her palm.

"I was so worried I'd never see you again," she whispered. "I'm sorry I was so upset. What I told you, it would've been difficult for anyone to accept. I should have been more patient, given you the time you needed."

He shook his head and took her hand in his before playing with her fingers. "You don't need to apologize. I do. You told me something important, and I should have believed you. From the moment I met you—"

"Held me at gunpoint," she teasingly corrected.

He let out a soft laugh. "Held you at gunpoint," he corrected, "I knew you were different. Special. You were unlike any woman I'd ever met, and I love that about you. I love that you were panning for gold out there all alone, dressed like a man. I love that you are brave and strong. I love that you go after what you want, that you fight for what you believe in. Every day I have known you, you've surprised me, impressed me, and have only made me fall deeper in love with you."

Gemma's heart fluttered. "You love me?"

He looked deep into her eyes. "I do. I love you so much, Gemma. When I saw you on the floor, unmoving, I thought I'd lost you. If I had, I would have never recovered. I love you so much I ache when you're away. I think of you every moment and look forward to the time when I can be with you again. I should have believed you when you told me. I'm sorry for that. But I believe you now."

Surprise filled her. "You do?"

He nodded. "Yes. It just makes sense—it explains everything. I don't need proof. You're proof enough."

Her heart overflowed with love, and she wrapped her arms around his neck. "I love you, Logan. I've looked my entire life for you, but it took me traveling back over two hundred years to find you. I'm so glad I did."

Unable to hold back another moment, she pressed her lips to his.

He let out a relieved sound then brought his hands to her head and kissed her back. "I love you," he whispered between kisses, telling her with his words and lips how much he truly meant it.

He finally pulled back. "Marry me, Gemma. I don't know if you want to stay with me or go back to your time. But whatever you choose, let me be with you."

Her eyes watered. The love shining from his eyes was everything she'd ever dreamed of. "Yes. You're everything I want, everything I'll ever need. My life is here, with you."

He grinned in happy relief, and then kissed her again, sealing their promise. "Then we'll stay here and build our future. I know how much you're giving up to be with me, but I promise I'll try to give you even more in return."

"As long as you love me, it will always be enough."

The look he gave her made her stomach flip.

"You'll never, ever need to doubt my love for you. I'll be sure to show you every single day."

She sighed into another kiss. She couldn't imagine ever being happier than this—in this time or the future.

All her dreams had come true.

EPILOGUE

Gemma looked at herself in the mirror one last time. Her white satin and lace gown was exquisite, more beautiful than any wedding dress she'd ever imagined.

"You look beautiful."

She gasped and spun toward the doorway. "Logan! What are you doing here? I told you we weren't supposed to see each other before the wedding!" She laughed.

"I couldn't stay away." He stepped into her room, leaving the door open, and came to her. "I wanted to see you, to tell you one more time that I'm so glad you're mine. I'm so glad you're marrying me. I'm the luckiest man alive." He lifted her hand and kissed the skin.

Need rushed through her. "I'm so glad too."

A glint entered his eye. "Just wait until tonight. I'll make you even happier."

Shocked, her mouth hung open, and she covered his mouth with her hand. "Oh my gosh!" She looked around to make sure no one else was in the room. "Someone could hear you."

Humor danced in his eyes, and he pressed a kiss to her

palm. They'd waited a month to get married, much longer than she'd wanted to, but Alison had begged them to let her plan a large event. "They'll hear us tonight."

Her cheeks colored. She knew he was probably right, but she didn't like thinking about it. She wanted to tease him again, but he just looked so happy. She felt like she'd waited forever to get to this day. "I'm so glad it's finally here."

"Me too," he whispered, kissing her lips before pulling away. "I also came to see if you were ready for the ceremony to start."

She sucked in a deep breath. "Just about." She was thrilled it was finally time, but there was a small part of today that was bittersweet.

Logan lifted her chin so she was looking at him. "Gemma, what is it? Is something wrong?"

She reached up and wrapped her hand around his wrist, holding it in place. "No. I'm so happy about today. It's just, I wish my dad was here."

She'd shown him pictures of her father, of her old home, her friends, and everything else she'd loaded to her phone so she'd never forget.

Understanding lit in his eyes, and he gathered her in his arms. "I know. I can't imagine how hard that must be. But you know he loves you. I'm sure he's thinking of you all the time."

She knew it was true. She'd tried to explain everything in her letter, but she knew her dad must still miss her. "I know. I don't miss anything else from the future except for him—and maybe pizza—but I can live without that."

"Maybe someday you'll see him again."

She ached, wishing that were true. "I know. I just...I wish my father were here for the wedding."

A loud crash sounded downstairs, a scream following right after. Gemma's eyes widened. "What was that?"

Logan was already moving toward the door. "Stay here."

"Uh. No way."

He threw her a resigned look as if he really wished she'd listen to him but knew she wouldn't. "If there's trouble, I want you to run back to your room and lock the door."

She didn't respond. If there was trouble, she would stay and protect him. She was never going to leave his side.

They made it downstairs, and the screaming stopped. But as they raced down the hall, they saw Alison pointing a gun at something in the library. "Who are you, and what do you want?"

Her weapon never wavered. Had someone broken into the house? Today of all days. It couldn't possibly be one of the guests, could it?

A male voice floated out of the room. "My name is Edward Watts. I'm Gemma Watts' father."

Alison lowered her gun. "Gemma's father?" She looked over her shoulder, seeing Logan and Gemma, but Gemma couldn't respond.

She knew that voice. Had missed it. Had heard it on her phone as she watched videos over and over.

She stepped into the doorway. "Dad?"

Relief crossed her father's face, and she rushed toward him, running into his arms. "Gemma! Are you all right?"

Tears sprang to Gemma's eyes. She couldn't hold them back if she tried. "I'm good. Everything is fine. How are you here? What happened? Did Dr. Lachele send you?" She asked him questions faster than he could respond.

He pulled back from her, looking at her face as if he couldn't believe he was actually seeing her. "When I got your letter, I couldn't believe it. I tried to track you down on your trip, but then I found out you hadn't left. I searched everywhere before finally approaching Dr. Lachele. She assured me you were well and that you had gotten married and were happy." He looked down at her white dress, a question in his eyes.

In her excitement, she'd completely forgotten about Logan and Alison and the wedding. "I'm not married yet."

Logan stepped forward. "But she will be in an hour." He nodded to her father. "I'm grateful you were able to make it in time, Mr. Watts. Gemma was heartbroken thinking about getting married without you here. I'm Logan Walburn." He offered his hand, and her father shook it tentatively, glancing at Gemma.

Logan held his hand out to Alison. "And this is my mother, Alison Walburn."

Her dad nodded in greeting toward Alison. "It's a pleasure to meet you. Do I have you both to thank for keeping an eye on my daughter?"

Alison set her weapon aside and stepped forward. "It been a pleasure having her here. We're so excited for her to join our family." She offered him her hand, and he took it, holding it gently. "And Mr. Walburn?" he asked, glancing around. "Is he here as well?"

Alison looked down. "He passed when Logan was young."

Regret crossed her father's features. "I'm sorry."

"It was a long time ago," she said.

Understanding passed between their two parents. Gemma had told Logan and Alison all about how her mother had abandoned them when she was small.

"Mr. Watts," Logan said, and everyone turned toward him. "I hadn't the opportunity to ask you this before, but considering I'm marrying your daughter in a few minutes, I'd like to have your blessing."

His eyes glanced at Gemma's white dress again. "Are you sure you want to get married right now, honey?"

She grinned and walked over to Logan, threading her arm with his. "Yes. I love him, Dad. He's everything I've ever hoped for. I know you just met him, but once you get to know him, you'll know that too."

Her dad looked between them, and then his stance relaxed. "I can see that already. And I can see how much you both love each other." He looked at Logan. "Yes. You have my permission to marry."

Gemma rushed back to her dad and hugged him. "Thank you so much." She pulled away and looked at him. "How long can you stay?"

He pointed to the bags behind him. "Forever."

Gemma's jaw dropped. "You're staying forever? You're not going back? What about your practice? What about the house?"

Her father smiled. "All taken care of. Gemma, there was nothing keeping me there. Sure, I had the dental practice, but I didn't care about it. You're the only thing in my life that means anything. I want to see you get married and have kids. I want to know my grandchildren."

Gemma's eyes watered again. She was so emotional! "Dad, I don't want you to give everything up for me."

He shook his head. "I did it for me. I needed a change. An adventure. The Wild West seemed like the perfect place. Besides, I did some research on dental care in this time period...I think people here will appreciate my skills."

She laughed through her water-logged eyes. "I love you so much, Dad."

"I love you too, sweetheart." He pulled away. "I forgot. I have a letter for you from Dr. Lachele."

"Dr. Lachele?"

He nodded and pulled it out of his coat pocket. "She said you'd be busy and could read it later." He shook his head as he handed it over. "She failed to mention you were busy *getting married*. She told me that if for some reason you decided to return back to your time, all you needed to do was click your heels three times and say, 'I wish to go home.'" He shook his head wryly. "She's quite the character."

Gemma chuckled. "She really is."

Her father smiled and sighed happily. "Now that that's done, and it doesn't look like you'll be a runaway bride, I think it's time for you to get married."

Gemma didn't know how she could be any happier than she was in this moment. "Thanks, Dad."

She gave her father one more hug before Alison stepped forward. "Why don't you come with me, Edward? I think one of Logan's suits will fit you just fine."

He smiled at Alison in a way Gemma had never seen. "That's very kind of you." He offered her his arm. "Shall we?"

A bemused expression filled Alison's face, and she blushed, taking his offered arm before Gemma's dad led her out of the room.

Logan smiled, watching their parents leave the room. "I think my mother is going to enjoy having a modern man around. He'll appreciate who she is instead of being intimidated by her."

Gemma agreed. It surprised her that their parents seemed to have an instant connection. She looked at Logan and smiled. "Maybe there's something that happens to us Watts when Walburns hold us at gunpoint. Instant love."

He snorted and then captured her in his arms. "It must be true." He kissed her. "I love you, Gemma."

She sighed, relaxing into the kiss. "I love you too."

"I think it's about time we got married."

"You don't know how long I've been waiting for that to happen."

He grinned. "Oh, I think I do."

He tucked her arm in his, leading her toward their future.

She never knew life could be so perfect or that she could

ever be so happy. She'd come here, hoping to find a love like this, one that could compare to the novels she read.

She just hoped all her friends had found the same thing. This was her happily-ever-after. And she'd always be grateful for her matchmaking fairy godmother.

Sunkissed

My Only Wish

Collaborations

Kitty: Bride of Hawaii (American Mail-Order Brides)

Falling for a Duke (Timeless Regency Collection)

Zara's Zephyr (The Alphabet Mail-Order Brides)

The Minx Miner (The Book Club)

The Witches of Redwood Falls

The Witching Moon (The Witches of Redwood Falls – Book 1)

The Witches Craft (The Witches of Redwood Falls – Book 2)

Discover other titles by Janelle Daniels

www.JanelleDaniels.com

Connect with me online.

I love to hear from readers!

Facebook:

https://www.facebook.com/groups/411789749214006/

Pinterest:

http://pinterest.com/JDanielsRomance/boards/

Twitter:

https://twitter.com/_JanelleDaniels

THE MINX MINER

Dream Cache Publishing

This is a work of fiction. Names, characters, places, and incidents either are products of the author's imagination or are used fictitiously. Any resemblance to actual events or locales or persons, living or dead, is entirely coincidental.

www.janelledaniels.com